I0627865

Little Lost #6

Charity Parkerson

Punk & Sissy Publications

Copyright

—Warning: This book is intended for readers over the age of 18. Some of my books contain allusions to past abuse and trauma.

CONTENTS

INTRODUCTION

*HE'S THE MOST HATED **and dangerous man in town. The only good thing he's ever done for this world is his sons. That probably won't change.***

Beau is the biggest weapons dealer on the west coast. He built an empire from the ground up. Having the world at his fingertips, and giving the world to his family, cost him everything. He went from having a beautiful life to having a drug-addicted wife and son. Then he lost it all, except the money that brings no warmth. He's bitter and done. That's not a good combination for someone as deadly as him. There's only one person who doesn't fear him or look at him with disgust. Kylo has no idea how much danger he's in.

Kylo lives in his head. Always has. For the most part, that's fine. He doesn't have any responsibilities, so he's free to be his Little self. The only area he's lacking is his love life. There aren't many men out there searching for someone strange like him. It's one thing to be a Little, but to also be odd is too much for most people. Beau looks at him in a way no one else ever has. It's too bad the guy could get him killed. He's not the first.

King Daddy is the sixth book in Charity Parkerson's Little Lost series where adorable, sometimes bratty, and scared Littles meet the men of their dreams.

Author Note

THIS SERIES IS A darker daddy/Little series. There's murder, suicide, and abuse along with heavy drug use. These are truly daddy/Little books with everything that entails. They won't be for everyone.

CHAPTER ONE

IT FELT STRANGE TO go from every day being high drama to absolute silence. That was how it was for Beau since his wife of nearly thirty years had committed suicide. Her addictions had won. Beau had tried every desperate move anyone could make to save her. He had also done his best to totally crush her when he needed her to feel the pain she caused others. By others, he really meant him. As sad as it made him, he hated her now. Everything he once loved had turned against him because she was weak, and he obviously was too. He had let all that bullshit happen. Now, life was just silent. Truthfully, he didn't even know what to do with himself any longer.

His meeting at the shipyard had gone perfectly. Thousands of weapons were on their way to some war-torn country. He lost track. Beau had even more money and soul-crushing stillness. Only his fight to reclaim the love of his sons gave him purpose. Beau wasn't sure that made any progress either. Life was simply empty and quiet, so fucking quiet.

His gaze slid toward the window as they waited for the light to turn green. Not a single guard made a sound. It was as if the emptiness of his life had muted everyone and everything around him. It was exhausting. Outside the window, a tiny blond struggled with a collapsible cart. His rage was evident as he fought to get the thing open. A smile tugged at the corners of Beau's mouth. He recognized the crazily dressed sprite.

"Pull into this lot."

No one ever questioned an order from him, and Beau didn't explain himself. A burning need lit in his chest, dispelling the quiet. He had met Kylo once at his son's club, The PlayPen. Kylo had been dangerously unafraid of Beau, unwittingly saving Beau at his lowest. He had given Beau a crown. His outfit was almost as wild today as it had been that night. He still wore a tutu over pants, but this one was black. The pants were too, so it didn't look quite as wild as Kylo obviously was. Beau had thought about him more than he should have, but he hadn't known where to even begin a search for him. All he had was a first name. Kylo should be terrified of how happy Beau was to see him again.

As the SUV rolled to a stop next to the open door of the Beamer where Kylo raged at his inanimate object, Beau stepped out, buttoning his dress jacket as he went. Without a word, he grabbed the cart from Kylo and easily popped it open with the push of a button.

"It was locked."

"King Boo!"

Beau felt the way his smile grew. When Kylo had crowned him, he had dubbed Beau King Boo. Beau couldn't let Kylo get away this time without a proper name exchange. "It's Beau, actually."

"Beau Actually is an odd name."

Despite himself, Beau's smile refused to budge. "Does this smart-ass act win you a lot of friends?"

Kylo's blue eyes took on a faraway look, as if he had turned inward. Beautiful eyes were one weakness of his. A bright smile exploded across Kylo's face. "Not really, no."

Beau shook his head. He was every bit as entertained as he had been the first time they met. "Why were you kicking a cart's ass when we drove by?"

Kylo blushed. Beau hadn't thought that possible considering he wore a black leather vest over a hot pink shirt with no purpose. "I need to get my groceries upstairs and I don't want to make more than one trip."

"I can help." Beau had no fucking clue why he had offered such a thing. He had people for that. It was Kylo. Beau wanted any excuse to stay in his odd company.

Kylo reached behind him and grabbed his keys from an open hidden purse beneath the vest. "You can unlock my door, if you'd like."

Beau's brain had moved way beyond that topic. "What the fuck, Kylo? You're bleeding."

He glanced down. "Oh, yeah. A guy tried to mug me earlier. He stabbed me."

The way Beau's brain lagged like an outdated computer was real. Kylo was so blasé about getting stabbed. It enraged him. How dare anyone touch this angel? "For fuck's sake." He made a gesture in the air and his security poured from the SUV. "Where is this guy?"

Kylo shrugged. "I don't know. Outside the grocery store where I left him, I suppose."

"Which store?" Beau heard the bite in his tone.

Kylo obviously didn't. "Only Organics on Wriley."

With a nod toward one of his men, two of his guys climbed back inside the SUV and drove away. He pointed at another. "Get the groceries inside." Beau focused on the last guard. "Take Kylo's car and pick up the doctor."

There was only one doctor used by his family. He knew Mickey would know who he meant. His closest guards had been with him for ages. Beau rarely had to ask for anything.

"Kylo, give Mickey your car fob."

Kylo dug through his bag and came out with the fob. He passed it over without question. Henry finished unloading the groceries and headed for the door.

Beau swept Kylo off his feet and followed. The upscale apartment building had a doorman, so there was at least that. Beau focused on him as he scrambled to open the door for him. "I have a man named Mickey returning with a doctor. Don't block their path."

Showing a serious lack of good judgment, the guy's dark gaze slid Kylo's way, silently asking permission.

"Please and thank you, Stew. I got hurt."

Stew immediately transformed from guard dog to kicked puppy. "Oh no. Is there anything else I can do?"

Kylo shook his head. "No, but I grabbed you a donut from the store. I'll have to bring it to you later."

Stew nodded. "You're amazing, but don't worry about me. Just get better."

Beau ground his back teeth as he swept Kylo inside. "Which floor?" He forced the words past his rage. Beau worried about Kylo, while it seemed like the guy didn't have the sense to worry about himself.

"Fifteen. It's the farthest elevator. That's the only one that goes that high, and you catch more flies with honey."

A loud snort burst from Beau and Henry. They exchanged a wry look. "Honey doesn't exist in my world."

"This isn't your world."

Damn. Kylo was either brave or stupid. Beau leaned toward brave, considering he was stabbed and still unafraid of Beau. He obviously had fight.

It turned out Henry had to use a key to take the elevator to Kylo's floor. At least the guy seemed to have decent security. When they reached the fifteenth floor, Henry and he exchanged glances again. The door opened directly into a gorgeous penthouse. It was the entire floor of the building. He had... questions. Beau shifted Kylo's weight slightly to get through the door.

Kylo gasped. It was the first indication he had given that he was in pain.

Beau automatically dropped his gaze. He studied Kylo's expression. It was obvious Kylo fought to stay upbeat, but his eyes swam with agony. Beau rushed toward the couch without looking anywhere else. He knew Henry was bright enough to find a kitchen and unload groceries without being told.

Kylo chuckled. "I'll bet you didn't have this on your bingo card for the day."

Despite everything, a smile exploded across Beau's face. Kylo made it impossible to be any other way. "I didn't, but such is life." He pushed the leather vest away and lifted Kylo's shirt. It was definitely much worse than Kylo had let on. He imagined only Kylo's black pants and shoes hid how much blood he had lost. Henry appeared with a towel. Beau tried to distract Kylo while he pressed it against the wound, putting pressure on it to stop the bleeding. "This is a nice place. It makes me realize how little I know about you."

Kylo visibly worked to draw a slow breath through his nose. When he spoke, it sounded like it was through clenched teeth. "You weren't up to talking to me the night we met."

That was true. Beau's ex had just rejected his pleas for a second chance. Nothing good could have come from them that night. It had been six months now. Beau hadn't forgotten the kindness this sprite had shown him when it mattered the most. He wouldn't leave him in this mess.

"Woo. My head is spinning."

His lips looked pale. A thought occurred to Beau. "Were you attacked before or after you got groceries?"

Kylo closed his eyes, as if he couldn't handle watching the room spin any longer. "I was on my way inside."

Beau's eyes automatically sought Henry. They held each other's stare in disbelief. "Text Mickey. Let him know you'll meet him outside so he can get up the elevator. Tell him to make sure the doctor brings blood."

Henry gave him a sharp nod.

"Would you take Stew his donut? He's always so good to me." Kylo didn't open his eyes as he made the request.

Beau fought not to look Henry's way again. Kylo sounded weak as hell, and he still worried about the goddamn doorman. On his knees beside the couch, Beau did his best to fight the demons. Memories of finding Tabitha, bleeding and with no hope of survival, poured through his head. It got harder to breathe. All he saw was the blood that covered the walls.

"My last name is Jinko. What's yours?"

A wry smile pulled at Beau's lips. This guy was amazing. It was obvious he tried to keep Beau calm, even in his state. He wasn't ready for Kylo to realize who he was. Beau needed to help him before Kylo tossed him out. A good person like Kylo wouldn't want a weapons dealer in his life. "Jinko? Like the pop singer? Pride Jinko?" Normally, Beau wouldn't have known that, but he was bisexual. No one fucked anyone their same sex and didn't know Pride Jinko. She was the face of gay-centric music since a time when it had been dangerous to be so bold.

Kylo chuckled. "Yeah, exactly like that. She's my mom."

Ah. High dollar car and apartment thoroughly explained. The way he dressed made more sense too. His mom was also known for being eccentric. "I can't imagine what that childhood must've been like."

"What was your childhood like?"

Panic was more than setting in. It had Beau locked down tight. "Poor and hungry."

"You have a nice accent."

"I was born in Italy." He also tried hard to kill his accent and roots, but it was hard when his emotions were high.

The elevator dinged, and Beau nearly cried out in relief. A tall, fit blond man in his forties poured from the lift, followed by Beau's guards, who were all laden with supplies. Beau moved aside, letting Dr. Fowler do his job.

"You must be Kylo."

Kylo opened his eyes at Dr. Fowler's words. "Hi. Yeah. Sorry to pull you away from whatever."

Beau shook his head.

Dr. Fowler chuckled. It was a deep yet soft sound. "It's my job. I'm Dr. Fowler. You can call me Austen, if that makes you more comfortable. I need to take a look at your wound."

Kylo nodded and closed his eyes again, as if the motion was too much.

Austen lifted the towel.

Beau eyed him, searching for any sign he made the pain worse than it already was.

"This might sound like a weird request, but I promise I have a good reason. Is it okay if we take off your shoes?"

"Of course. Do whatever you need."

Fuck. He sounded bad.

Austen carefully took off Kylo's shoe, as if anticipating exactly what happened. Blood poured out. He straightened and immediately set to work. Beau got out of the way and watched from across the room. Austen had Mickey and Rico in surgical gloves and helping. He started an IV while Mickey hung a bag of blood from the IV pole he had just pieced together. Austen pulled a shot from his pocket and stuck it in the IV line. "I'm just injecting a little saline first, so you'll feel a little rush of cold." He did that, then immediately pulled a second shot from the pocket of his doctor's coat. "This one is for pain. It'll send heat through your veins, but you should feel relief almost immediately."

From there, Austen was on his knees, tearing into more things from his pockets. "First, I'll deaden the skin, but it won't help completely with the numbing until after a few sticks. Sorry about that, but I need to feel around for damage, and I don't want you to feel that any more than you have to."

Kylo never responded.

That had Beau moving to where Kylo's head rested on the end of the couch. He kneeled and swiped his fingers through Kylo's hair. It was so light but also obviously his natural color.

Kylo reached up and grabbed his hand.

Beau's throat swelled. Kylo was incredibly tough and brave. He felt Kylo's grip loosen, and his hand slipped away.

Beau's panicked gaze shot to Austen. "Good. He's passed out. He did not want to be awake for this." Austen stuck his fingers inside the wound and felt around. His light blue eyes looked completely focused on his work.

Henry touched Beau's shoulder, pulling his attention away. He held out a phone. "You should see this."

Reluctantly, Beau stood and accepted the device. A video was cued up. Beau tapped the screen, starting it. It was security footage from the store. Beau didn't ask how he got it. His men were the best. He watched as what looked to be a homeless man jumped Kylo. In one swift move, Kylo had the guy flipped over his shoulder and on the ground. Unfortunately, drug-fueled rage was real. He had seen it with Tabitha a million times. The guy was immediately back on his feet. He lunged at Kylo, stabbing him. Beau winced. No doubt that was a disgusting knife. Kylo's hand shot out. He used the lower part of his palm, exactly like someone trained would, driving it straight into the guy's nose. Without missing a beat, his knee landed in the guy's gut. He used the momentum to throw him to the ground. Kylo stepped over him and went inside the store as if nothing had happened.

Beau shook his head. "This guy."

Henry chuckled. "Right? What the fuck?" The pride-filled laugh matched the feeling in Beau's chest. Kylo was one tough cookie.

"I need more light."

At his pronouncement, everyone scrambled, looking for anything that could be used. Henry rolled his eyes, turned on the flashlight on his phone, and moved to hold it over Austen's shoulder like a kid helping his dad work on a car.

Despite everything, Beau smiled. Kylo would be fine. He was obviously one tough Little. Plus, Beau was here. He would make sure Kylo got whatever he needed. Kylo had once saved his sanity. Beau owed him for that. He paid his debts.

The cotton mouth was new. Kylo usually was pretty good at staying hydrated. He
didn't drink, but he imagined this was what
a hangover felt like. His eyelids didn't want
to lift. He felt weird—like overly exhausted
and weak. Kylo didn't get sick often. This
felt like the flu. He forced his eyes to open.
His gaze slid around the room. He was in
bed. An IV bag hung over his head. Red liq-
uid headed toward his arm. Oh yeah. The
homeless guy. How exhausting.

He peered over the edge of the bed. Yep.
The IV pole had wheels. He needed to pee
and then find out if the handsome doctor
was still here. Kylo hated the thought of
having to remove an IV alone. He sat up,

gritting his teeth and trying not to scream at the tearing sensation in his gut. He wore his mouse pajamas. Kylo didn't remember changing clothes. Carefully, he padded to the bathroom. He winced when he flipped on the light and caught a glimpse of his reflection. There were dark circles under his eyes. Poor Beau. He always showed up when Kylo was at his worst. The first time they met, Kylo had been having a bit of a meltdown. This wasn't much better.

Kylo ran through the usual morning routine of emptying his bladder, washing his hands, and brushing his teeth. He didn't know if it was morning or night. The familiar routine helped him feel a little more human. As he slowly made his way from the bedroom, he was engulfed in total darkness. That was pretty par for course for his bedroom. He kept the blackout curtains drawn, but he never turned off his kitchen light. Kylo couldn't see shit.

He carefully shuffled his way to the kitchen, trying not to trip over anything or run his IV pole into anything.

"Why are you up?"

The groggy-sounding question startled him, but not horribly. He had doubted they would leave him with an IV in and all their equipment without someone to help.

Kylo felt around until he found the light switch and turned on the kitchen light. It was always the best choice since the wall, doorway, and light fixture were perfectly aligned to only give a soft glow to the living room.

Beau was stretched out on the couch.

Kylo couldn't help the smile that snapped to his lips at the sight of him, sleep-mussed and looking like the sexy daddy he was. "Hey. You could've slept with me or even in one of the guest rooms."

"I don't sleep with people when they can't consent, and I wanted to be here in case you did exactly this."

Beau sat up. "What do you need?"

"I'm thirsty. Do you want anything?"

With a shake of his head, Beau stood. "Tell me what *you* want, and I'll bring it to you."

Kylo didn't budge. At tea parties, the host always served. He didn't know how to act.

"You have a pitcher of water in the fridge. Is that what you usually drink?"

"I don't like plain water. There are some of those flavor pack things in the cabinet next to the fridge. If you're interested," he tacked on because he still wasn't sure if he should host.

Beau padded his way. His feet were bare. Kylo had no idea why that caught his atten-tion. Both times he had seen Beau before now, he had been so put together. It seemed odd to see him relaxed.

"Come on. Back to bed. You're not supposed to be up until after the infusions."

"How much blood have I gotten?"

"A lot." Beau steered him toward the bed-room. With his arm around Kylo's waist. Kylo felt warm and safe. Beau talked as they walked. "You know, most people, when they get stabbed, go immediately to the hospital."

Kylo shrugged. "I had things to do."

Beau snorted. He turned on the light before he eased Kylo into bed and tucked him in. "When exactly did you plan to get help?"

He was getting a little irritated at the third degree. "As soon as I put up my groceries.

That's why I was so angry over the cart not opening. I've been taking care of myself for a while, you know." The irritation drained from him as quickly as it hit. Considering the way he had passed out not long after getting home, he probably would have died if Beau hadn't shown up when he did. "Maybe I'm not very good at it, but—so far—I've kept myself alive."

"I know. It's okay to relax now. You have help."

The claim nearly cracked Kylo, even though he would never show it. He had spent his life alone. "Thank you. After you get something to drink, you're welcome to sleep with me."

"I appreciate it."

Kylo stared at the ceiling when Beau walked away. He was in a lot of pain. Someone was being nice to him, and he felt vulnerable as hell. He tried to breathe through the discomfort in his chest and gut.

Beau returned with a bright red drink, proving he had put extra drink mix in the water. "Let's get you sat up for a minute so you can drink this and take some pain meds."

Kylo tried not to show his relief. Unfortunately, it laced his voice. "Thank you."

Beau sat on the edge of the bed and watched him take the pain pill. "You're tough as nails. Most people would be crying right now, and you handled that guy who attacked you like a champ."

The pain made him weepy, and he said too much. Kylo settled back on the pillows and closed his eyes. "I have a famous mom. That meant I raised myself except for the security and private tutors she hired for me. My favorite guard, Gary, taught me how to defend myself. He knew I would be alone as soon as I got grown. Boy, was he right," Kylo muttered under his breath.

"It looks like your mom has kept you financially safe."

Kylo took a slow breath, praying the fire in his gut eased. There was something in Beau's voice. "Do you have kids?"

"Yes. Two sons."

Ah. He obviously kept his sons in the high life while barely seeing them. That was the tone he had heard. Another parent who thought parenting meant buying shit. "Do you see them?" Kylo knew he dug and was being nosey. More than anything, he needed something to focus on while waiting for the meds to kick in.

"Sometimes. My youngest owns The PlayPen."

With his eyes still closed, Kylo smiled. "It's good you still support him, even with him owning a kink club."

"I was there for a reason the night I met you, so I can't judge, can I?"

Kylo finally opened his eyes and focused on Beau. Holy hell. It was obvious Beau hadn't expected him to open his eyes. The heat that stared at him—until Beau rearranged his features—scorched him to his soul.

Kylo had never been a wilting butterfly. He gave the heat right back. "Good to know you weren't just visiting your son. That means I have a shot."

"Go to sleep."

"Or not," Kylo muttered as Beau turned out the light.

He felt the bed dip. Kylo listened as Beau shuffled around, getting comfortable. Truth be told, he didn't know why he flirted with Beau. The guy was obviously someone important. Kylo hadn't missed the way he had dodged giving his last name. He was probably married or something. Fuck. He had two sons. There was a very real chance he had a wife at home. Well, shit. Life was always a kick right in his ass. Beau had made a singular mistake, though. He had told him about his son owning The PlayPen. Now he was an internet search away from Kylo knowing all about him.

CHAPTER TWO

NONSTOP THOUGHTS ABOUT KYLO had Beau sitting at The PlayPen more often, hoping his little kung fu master showed. He kept to himself unless he spotted one of his sons. Beau knew they didn't see it or appreciate it, but he tried his ass off to fix their family. It wasn't like him to go out of his way for people. His family meant everything to him, whether they realized it or not.

His sons-in-law played nearby with the husband of his youngest son's bodyguard. He knew Banks thought of his guard, Shane, more like a brother than an employee. That sometimes happened with longtime employees. Henry had been with him since Beau began his business back in Italy. The guy wasn't allowed to walk away.

His sons, on the other hand, were a hairsbreadth away from never looking back. Today, surprisingly, they sat with him, watching their husbands take turns jumping on a small trampoline. Briefly, he considered using Henry's upcoming birthday as an excuse to ask them to dinner. He tossed the idea aside. They would probably just take Henry out without him. Plus, his ex had recommended not manipulating them. Kylo had said he caught more flies with honey. He had nothing to lose by taking their advice.

Beau cleared his throat. "The house has been really quiet without your mom. Would you two join me for dinner? Please?" He tacked on the last bit purely to prove Kylo wrong. Honey didn't work on people like them.

Boone and Banks looked his way.

Banks answered on their behalf. "Sure, Dad."

He was shocked, but he jumped on the agreement. "Is seven okay?"

Boone looked thoughtful. "Can we do six instead? Jupiter has a dentist appointment in the morning. I'd like to get him to bed early."

Beau stood before they changed their minds. "Six is great. I should probably head out, though, so I can let Pierre know."

"I do miss Pierre's cooking." Banks made the claim while watching his husband. He sounded distracted, but Beau would take it.

"See you at six." He headed for the door. There was a bit of pep in his step. He felt like he had found a new superpower. Beau had

Mickey stop by their favorite coffeehouse and grab some pastries before heading to Kylo's place. He had no intention of telling Kylo he had been right. Beau just wanted to see him. He wanted to make sure he was healing okay.

With his bribe in hand, Beau headed Stew's way. "Good afternoon, Stew. I'm just here to see Kylo." He acted as if he suddenly recalled the donuts he held. "Oh. I saw these and knew Kylo would want you to have them."

A bright smile stretched the burly doorman's face. "Thank you. These are my favorite. Kylo isn't home, though. He's never here on Thursdays."

Beau tried his best to hide his disappointment. It seemed honey wasn't as potent as Kylo claimed. "That's too bad. I'll have to check back another day."

Stew nodded. "Try back tomorrow. He's always at home on Fridays."

Well, he would be damned. He had bribed the guy right into telling Kylo's schedule.

Beau smiled. "Thanks. I'll do that. Have a great day."

"You as well, sir."

Well, fuck. Now he had the whole day to kill before the boys came for a visit. He ended up sitting on the couch and staring at the crown Kylo gave him. It truly was beautiful. It belonged on Kylo's head. Not his. He hadn't stopped thinking about Kylo, saying he had a chance. Beau had panicked a little at the flirtation. Kylo didn't know him. He didn't see the monster. If he knew Beau, and—somehow—still accepted him, Beau would eventually have to confess all his sins. Kylo would look at him differently. The sassy smile would turn to disgust.

Maybe even hate. It was nice having one person in the world still think he was good.

Boone came through the door with Jupiter on his arm.

Beau set the crown aside and stood. He hadn't realized how long he had been lost in thought. "Hey. You made it. I don't think dinner is quite ready yet." At least Pierre hadn't said as much.

"It's fine. I'm a little early. Jupiter wanted to chat with Pierre about a recipe."

Beau motioned in the direction of the kitchen. "Feel free. I'm sure he'd love to see you." He had no idea if that was true, but Jupiter had gone to culinary school and apparently loved to cook. Since Boone seemed to encourage him, Beau kept his opinion to himself. As long as Jupiter didn't actually work, Beau didn't care about his hobbies.

Jupiter skipped off to the kitchen.

Boone moved to where Beau had been brooding all day. "Holy shit, Dad. Why is this just sitting on your couch instead of being in a display case or a fucking museum? How in the hell did you even get it?"

Beau blinked at Boone's over-the-top reaction. "What do you mean?"

Boone held the crown with reverence as he met Beau's stare. "This is the famous three-million-dollar crown Alexander the Mighty, King of Argetta, made for his affair son. It caused an uproar since Argetta is such a poor country, its people struggling, while he threw money at things like this for a kid who would never even be king." Boone turned it from side to side and eyed the crown. "Damn. The history books did not do it justice. It really is gorgeous."

Beau didn't know what to say or how to react. "Maybe it's a reproduction."

Boone flashed a smile his way. "One thing I know is craftsmanship. These are real jewels and this was made by a master."

Damn. Kylo hadn't known him at all when he had simply given Beau the crown. Beau swallowed. "I didn't know. It was given to me by a friend."

"That's a hell of a friend." Boone set the piece on the table. "You might want to at least put that in the safe."

"I have a spot for it." And an excuse to see Kylo. Things were looking up.

*

Unknown number: *As amazing as your security is, it makes visiting you irritating as hell.*

Kylo: *Do I know you?*

Unknown number: *It's Beau. I'm down-stairs.*

Kylo: *Go to the farthest elevator. I'll send it down for you.*

Kylo chewed his bottom lip and tried to decide how to stand while waiting for Beau. Maybe he should sit. It was possible stand-ing looked desperate. He rushed to sit on the couch. Kylo winced as his stitches pulled. He was so dumb sometimes. The lift dinged, and Beau stepped out. Kylo near-ly sighed. He was dressed casually tonight. Soft-looking black shirt and jeans. His gray hair was perfect—like he had a stylist at home. He was a lot older than Kylo. That was exactly what Kylo wanted.

"Hey. How did you get my number?"

Beau's smile was completely unrepentant. "It's probably best not to ask me how I find anything. I have my ways." He held an open box. Beau crossed the room and passed it Kylo's way. "You should probably have this back. I can't imagine why you'd give it to me in the first place." He claimed the spot on the couch next to Kylo while Kylo stared at the crown with his heart in his throat.

Kylo didn't touch it. He held the box out to Beau. "I crowned you king."

Beau didn't take it. "I won't take a priceless piece of history from you."

A wry smile tugged at Kylo's lips. He dropped the box on his lap. "I wouldn't say it's priceless. It obviously had a price tag, and it's also not that historical. Only about a hundred and fifty years, actually. As far as history goes, that's pretty recent."

"So it is real."

It wasn't a question. That gave Kylo the freedom to ignore the statement.

"If you have a safe, you should lock that up."

A smile snapped to Kylo's lips. "I couldn't even give it away. Now you're worried it'll get stolen."

Beau's serious expression never wavered. "No. I'm worried someone might hurt you to get it."

Someone had already murdered his soul to give it to him. "That's fair." Kylo stood and made his way to the bedroom.

Beau followed on his heels. He leaned his shoulder against the doorframe and watched as Kylo opened the safe and shoved it inside. "Are you really moving around as well as you appear, or are you faking it?" *The way you always do*. Kylo swore those unspoken words hung in the air.

"I've been taking the meds the doctor left for me. He told me what to look for, as far as infection, when he came to check on me early this morning. There's nothing to do but keep doing my thing. Life doesn't give a shit if you're hurting."

Beau nodded. "Yeah. Sounds about right." He straightened. "Anyhow. I just wanted to give that back to you."

A hint of panic soared through Kylo. It was obvious Beau intended to leave. Kylo wasn't ready to return to the silence. "Tell me what you did today."

Beau's mouth lifted in one corner. He was just so beautiful. Kylo wished he were beautiful. "Only if you tell me about your day. I came to see you earlier, and Stew said you're never home on Thursdays."

"Yet you came back. What made you think I'd be here the second time?"

He didn't answer right away. Kylo wondered if he was about to hear a lie. "It was more hope than anything."

Well, if it was a lie, it made him happy anyhow.

Beau closed the distance between them. He snagged the hem of Kylo's shirt. Kylo's heart sped. He just knew Beau had all the experience. Beau would probably do anything and do it well. He held Kylo's stare while he lifted Kylo's shirt.

"Have you been checking your wound for infection?"

Disappointment washed over him. He didn't reply. Kylo couldn't look away from his dark eyes. He had the appearance of a man who knew his worth. Kylo's throat swelled. Just like everyone, he didn't want Kylo.

"You're not wearing a tutu today."

"That can change, if you want?"

Beau didn't smile. His expression never shifted or gave a single thought away. "I want you to be uniquely you. It's refreshing."

"I'm in too much pain to dance today."

At his confession, Beau inspected his wound again. Kylo studied his face. Even the laugh lines at the corners of his eyes were sexy. "This is a little red."

"Would you like a drink?" Kylo didn't like being seen as weak in any way.

"I don't drink anymore." Beau's voice had turned strangely hard.

"Good. There isn't a drop of alcohol in this house." A nervous chuckle left his lips. "It just seemed like something a real adult would say."

Beau's features softened. "What would you say instead? I'd prefer that."

"Do you like being called Boo?"

"Not anymore." He didn't sound sad.

Kylo took that as a win. "I know you go to The PlayPen to visit your son, but do you like to be called daddy?"

Something dark and breathtaking sparked in Beau's eyes. "Very much." He paused and cocked his head to one side, studying Kylo. "What do you like to be called?"

Kylo smiled. He genuinely liked Beau. He opened his mouth to respond, and the phone rang. "Excuse me. That's the security line." Kylo headed for the phone with his heart in his throat. No one good could be waiting to see him. "Hello?"

"Mr. Reggie is here to see you."

Kylo's heart sped. His pulse beat in his ears. "He doesn't have my permission to come up."

A moment of silence met his words. Finally, the guard cleared his throat. "He's pretty insistent."

Kylo squeezed the phone, trying not to panic. "I don't give a damn what he is. He doesn't have my permission."

"Yes, sir."

Kylo dropped the phone back into place. He stared into space and strained to hear any sounds of the elevator moving. He paid a lot of money to live here for the best security. Kylo needed it to hold.

Hands squeezed his shoulders.

Kylo jumped and tried to hide his reaction with a smile.

Beau didn't call him on it. "I should let you get some rest."

Kylo wanted to beg him to stay for just a few more minutes. He couldn't do that. His fear couldn't be completely ignored. He still tried to play it cool. "Hey, I haven't thought to say this, but anytime you're on your way up, please don't allow anyone on the elevator with you. Most people don't even think about it. It's second nature to hold the door and let people share the ride. But obviously, this elevator opens to my home, so..."

Thankfully, Beau didn't look curious, or as if he felt chastised. He simply flashed a sexy smile. "Of course. You have my number now. Text me if you need anything."

"Thank you. I—" The phone rang again, cutting him off. "Sorry. Hold on." He fought the urge to snatch up the phone and scream. "Hello?"

"Dr. Fowler is here to see you."

Relief had a huge smile exploding across his face. "Send him up." Kylo sounded much happier than he should have. He simply couldn't handle any more of life's bullshit tonight.

"Yes, sir."

Kylo hung up the phone.

Beau studied him. For a moment, Kylo expected him to ask about the call. He went a different way. "I didn't know anyone had landlines anymore, especially someone your age."

Kylo laughed. "First off, it's not a regular landline. It's a security line. You can't make or receive calls or anything. Only talk to the front desk. Secondly, how young do you think I am?"

Beau shrugged. "Much younger than me. Otherwise, I don't have a guess. Everyone younger than me looks like they're twenty to me."

Kylo shook his head. "I'll walk you to the elevator. Dr. Fowler is on his way up."

A strange look passed over Beau's features before he hid it. "Good. He needs to look at your wound." They headed toward the lift. Beau chuckled. "So you're not even going to tell me your age after all that?"

Kylo thought about teasing him and re- fusing. But he wanted to know everything about Beau, so tit for tat. "I'm thirty-two."

Beau literally stopped mid step to turn his way. "You're joking. I seriously thought you were twenty. I just didn't want to say that."

A laugh burbled in Kylo's throat. "Thank you... I think." He couldn't stop smiling at Beau's genuine shock.

The elevator dinged, and the door slid open.

Austen looked a bit surprised to see Beau, but his smile seemed genuine. "Hey. On your way out?" he asked, holding the door.

Since they were standing right outside the elevator, it was a fair assumption. Still, Beau seemed a bit annoyed. The laughter in his eyes died. "It seems so." His gaze swung Kylo's way. "Remember what I said. Text if you need anything."

Kylo nodded. "I will. Thank you."

With a final nod at them both, Beau disappeared behind the closing door.

Kylo focused on Austen. "Hey. Twice in one day. I feel special."

A bright smile met his words. The good doctor was a sexy guy. He was probably in his mid-forties. Even though he was the typical blond hair and blue-eyed Californian hottie, the same could be said of Kylo. They would look good together. It was an odd thought. Kylo's head was always all over the place.

Austen motioned toward the elevator as they headed for the couch. "Some guy tried to jump in the elevator with me on my way up. I refused. Did I do the right thing? It seemed odd."

Affection washed over Kylo. Austen had protected him, even without knowing if he should. "Thank you so much. My mom is famous, and even though I don't know why that brings crazies to me, it does."

Austen nodded, looking serious, as if Kylo's words mattered. It warmed his chest. "I'll be vigilant from now on." He sounded like he planned to come back. "Anyhow, I stopped by because I thought about you all day." He paused as if rethinking his words. He laughed. "I thought about your injury all day. Last night, I pushed some antibiotics through your IV, but I'm not sure that's doing enough."

Kylo nodded along. "The wound is a little red."

Austen seemed to go on alert. "May I see it?"

"Sure." Kylo lifted his shirt.

Austen moved in close to inspect it. Kylo watched him. He looked smart and capable. Kylo wondered if he was someone's father. If so, were they proud? They should be.

"Do you have kids?" Kylo was a bit horrified by the question, but he didn't take it back. Austen was a stranger in his home, inspecting his stomach.

A sad-looking smile touched Austen's lips. His blue gaze flipped upward and held his stare. "No. I've chased a lot of relationships over the years. They were always faster," he added with a chuckle.

Kylo laughed too, but the words made him sad. Laughter always masked the pain of loneliness. It hurt to want people more than they wanted you. It made him sad to think of Austen wanting someone who treated him the way everyone treated Kylo.

"This doesn't look horrible, but I also don't like how it looks. Have you been trying to do too much?" Austen shook his head. "Don't answer that. You look exactly like someone who does too much."

A bark of laughter burst from Kylo. "What is that supposed to mean? I know how to follow doctor's orders... I just don't."

Austen roared with laughter. The sound made Kylo smile. Austen swiped at his eyes. "That's what I thought. Let me put some antibiotic ointment on this and then I'd like to give you a shot. I've also got some pills I'd like to leave you. We know nothing about the knife he used, and I'm sure it wasn't clean." Austen paused for a moment. "Actually, I should probably draw some blood too and run some tests. Just to be safe," he added, as if he didn't want Kylo to worry.

Kylo shrugged. "Whatever you feel is necessary. You're the doctor."

The laughter returned to Austen's eyes. "I'm the doctor you don't listen to."

Kylo's hands rose and fell. "To be fair, I don't listen to anyone."

Austen's laughter lightened the black mood that had threatened to swallow him since Reggie tried again to visit.

"Would you like to stay for dinner?"

Austen's smile never faltered. The happy light in his eyes never dimmed. "Sounds great."

Kylo took a breath. He would be okay. He would find his way. Kylo always did somehow.

CHAPTER THREE

Do you like to be called daddy? The question burned into Beau's brain, making his skin itch with a dark impatience. That, mixed with the way Austen had made Kylo smile, drove him insane. And who had tried coming up that elevator before the doctor? Kylo was just such a mystery to him. He didn't know if he shouldn't simply walk away. Kylo didn't belong in his world. He couldn't stop thinking about the panic in Kylo's voice over that unexpected visitor. Beau had left, hoping to catch the guy. He hadn't seen anyone who seemed desperate or out of place. Beau hadn't stopped worrying all night. It was ridiculous. He had to do something.

"Rico."

Rico snapped to attention. "Yes, sir."

"Shadow Kylo. See if you spot anyone else doing the same. Something is nagging at me."

"Yes, sir."

Rico headed for the door.

"Oh, and Rico, if you catch him, bring him to me."

"Yes, sir."

There. Beau had done his last good deed for Kylo. He could stop thinking about the guy. Beau needed to leave Kylo to the Austens of the world.

"You need to see this, Beau."

Beau sat up from his overly relaxed pose on the couch. Henry was the only guard allowed to call him by his first name. He didn't hear Henry excited often.

"What's up?"

"An armored truck with several guards special delivered a box." He handed a package to Beau. "All the dogs sniffed it. It's not a bomb or drugs."

Beau's brow furrowed. Only one thing was written on the outside: Beau Bosi. Beau pulled out his pocketknife and sliced open the box. In his business, it could be anything. He held his breath. A smile exploded across his face as he pulled back the flaps. It was the crown. Beau shook his head as he unfolded the note inside.

I dub thee King Daddy.

A bark of laughter burst from Beau. He pulled the crown from the box and eyed it. Damn. It was beautiful. The piece should definitely be on Kylo's head. Why did he keep giving it to Beau?

"This guy makes you smile in a way I haven't seen in decades."

If anyone other than Henry had said that he would've razed the place. Henry knew him.

Beau kept his gaze locked on the crown. "Why does a guy like Kylo continue to give me a priceless crown?"

Henry scratched the graying hair on his chin. "Maybe he wants you to bring it back? Like a way to keep seeing you."

That made as much sense as anything did. "I guess you'd better bring the SUV around, then."

The smile Henry wore told him everything he needed to know. Henry thought he'd made the right decision. Beau repacked the crown and gathered his things. As he stuffed his phone in his back pocket, he wondered if he should call first. He immediately dismissed the thought. Kylo might deny him. Beau just managed to lift his mood. He couldn't handle another drop right now. Beau had been on the edge of something ugly for a while now. He scared himself on a good day. There was no telling what he could do.

Two guards fell into step behind him as he headed out. Henry pulled up in the SUV. Impatience poured through his veins on the way to Kylo's. Ugly thoughts tried pushing their way in. What if the doctor had stayed the night? He couldn't think like that. Beau had chosen to leave last night. He could have stayed. Beau wasn't sure Kylo deserved that.

By the time he reached Kylo's place, he second-guessed his every move. Still, he headed Stew's way, wishing he had brought a bribe.

Stew smiled and dipped his chin in greeting. "Good afternoon." He opened the door for Beau and then followed him inside. "Mr. Jinko asked me to send you up anytime you stopped by." He used his keys to call for Kylo's elevator.

"Thank you. I appreciate your help." There. Kylo would be proud.

"Good day, Mr. Bosi."

He stepped into the elevator. The door slid closed, and it hit him. Kylo had written his full name on the box. His gaze dropped to it. His name stared back at him. How long had Kylo known him? Had he recognized him from the beginning? Discomfort crawled up his spine. He didn't know how to feel. On one hand, he didn't have to hide or lie. On the other, someone as sweet as Kylo pretended to be could never want someone like him in their life. Another voice whispered in the back of his mind. His sons had found the sweetest of men. What were the odds he would be as lucky? Not high.

The door opened, setting him free inside Kylo's apartment. It seemed empty. Stew hadn't said Kylo wasn't home. Surely, the guy wouldn't have sent him to Kylo's unoccupied apartment. He checked all the rooms, saving Kylo's bedroom for last. There was a possibility he was in the bathroom or resting. The bedroom was empty too. Beau stood in the bedroom doorway, confused as fuck. Then a hint of music caressed his ears. Beau followed the sound. The closet door stood open. Beau stepped inside. It was empty, but there was definitely music coming from inside. He moved deeper into the clothes and shoes. A sliver of light caught his attention. It peeked from beneath where the wall met the floor. He pushed. A hidden door swung inward. Music poured out. Beau stepped inside and froze.

The first time Beau had been to Kylo's apartment, he had puzzled over a few things. They met at The PlayPen. Kylo had worn pajamas like a Little would. He had presented as a Little in every way. Yet his apartment was devoid of anything the least bit childlike. In fact, it was perfectly decorated, as if put together by a professional. No one visiting him would see him as anything other than an ordinary man. This was different.

The first half of the expansive room was a dance studio—like a professional studio. The walls were mirrors. Bars lined the wall for stretching. A wood floor shone bright with the perfect polish. There was a section for a stuffed animal audience. The bear Beau had given Kylo the night they met was right up front. Beyond the dance floor looked to be a playroom. Beau wasn't sure. He couldn't look at anything except Kylo. Dressed like a ballerina, he glided around the room. It wasn't a child playing dress-up. He was a fucking pro. If Kylo hadn't performed on a major stage, Beau would throw a hundred grand in the street. He chose a chair up front with his bear and sat.

"Did you come to watch me dance, Daddy?"

Beau's throat swelled. He was beautiful. "Yes, baby."

Kylo didn't miss a step. He took another spin around the room before coming to a stop in front of Beau. His gaze dropped to the box Beau held. He flipped it open and lifted the crown from the box. Kylo gently placed it on Beau's head. "Dance with me, Daddy."

Beau had to swallow past the lump in his throat. "I'd make you look bad."

Kylo moved the box to an empty seat and took Beau's hands. "I promise you won't." He moved across the floor, sweeping Beau along with him. Beau stared at Kylo. He looked content. Almost dreamy. He caught glimpses of their reflection. Beau in his crown. Kylo in his tutu and tights. They looked perfect together. Something unfurled inside of Beau. Something he had put away a long time ago and sealed shut. Definitely something he hadn't been looking for. The music stopped. They did too. Neither of them pulled away.

"That crown was meant for you."

"Should you be doing this with your injury?"

He felt Kylo shrug. "I get sad without it."

Kylo felt so perfect in his arms. He couldn't let go. Not yet. "Why do you keep giving me this crown?"

Apparently, it was the wrong question. Kylo stepped out of his hold. He didn't meet Beau's gaze as he headed for a chair and sat like he was in pain. "Maybe I'm trying to break its curse."

Beau stood over Kylo and peeled the sleeves of his one-piece outfit down his arms. Blood seeped through the light pink piece. He kept going until he had the top half around Kylo's waist. Then he dropped to his knees at Kylo's feet and eyed the leaking wound. It would never get better at this rate.

"What curse?" He checked Kylo's stitches, hoping he would answer if Beau didn't meet his stare.

Kylo hissed as Beau pressed around the stitches to check if they had torn. He chuckled afterward. "It's the gift given in place of love. Everyone who has ever received that crown got it as a present from someone who felt guilty for not loving them. It's an expensive pacifier." Beau lifted his chin. Kylo's eyes were closed, and he breathed as if muscling through a silent suffering. "When I gave it to you that first time, I thought, there. It was a selfless gift given for only the purest of reasons. Maybe it'll finally be used for good." He laughed. "Then you gave it back to me. What am I even supposed to make of that?"

Beau had no idea what Kylo was talking about. He was more worried about the way Kylo seemed slightly out of his head. "I'll keep it safe and treasure the intent."

A sweet smile played on Kylo's lips. "Thank you."

Beau stood and plucked Kylo from the chair. "Now. Time to rest." He carried Kylo to bed.

Kylo didn't fight him, even as Beau untied and unwound his slippers. Beau kept talking, hoping to keep Kylo from arguing. "You look beautiful. How long have you done ballet?"

"As long as I can remember." A soft chuckle escaped him. "I thought if I was the best in the world, then Mom would see me. Remember I exist. I don't suppose she ever even noticed she paid for the lessons. An accountant was told to keep me happy and in the best of everything." Kylo went silent for a moment. When he spoke again, his voice was barely a whisper. "Is that love? Is pouring money into someone all there is? Maybe I'm the failure."

Kylo's skin was on fire. Beau had a bad feeling infection had set in, and Kylo would be horrified when his fever broke. Despite the reason for their conversation, Beau was intrigued. His kids felt the same. Beau knew they did. He had given them money and pain. That was it. He couldn't take it back and he didn't know how to fix any of it. There was no way they could see how young he had become a father, a husband, and a master criminal. Tabitha and he had been sixteen when she became pregnant with Boone. Their parents had immediately seen them married, emancipating them and leaving them to figure out how to survive. His sons would never know what it was like for him to not know what the hell he was doing while he failed at everything but being bad. Beau was a fucking maestro at crime. He had no excuses. There would be no forgiveness from the people he loved the most. He was no better than the people who broke Kylo's heart. Still, he found himself talking as he undressed Kylo, saying all the things.

"People think parents are handed a baby, and all the world's knowledge zaps into their heads. That's not what happens. We do a lot of panicking, second-guessing ourselves, and trying our damnedest not to make the same mistakes our parents did. Meanwhile, we're just fucking our kids up in whole new ways. I bet, if you asked, you'd learn your mom grew up dirt poor and resenting her parents for all they couldn't give her. So she went hardcore in the opposite direction with you. I know that's where I went wrong." Beau paused and stared at nothing. "They didn't turn out like you, though. Their hatred looks a lot different."

"I don't hate my mom. I'd have to know her to hate her. It's more of a resentment-filled indifference while sitting in the quietest home in existence." He chuckled. "I guess that sounds pathetic. Maybe I should stop talking."

Without thinking, Beau kissed the ankle he unwrapped. "It's not pathetic. It's painfully familiar." He straightened. "I need to call Austen. Just rest, please."

With his eyes closed, Kylo nodded.

Beau pulled out his phone and headed for the living room. His heart had felt heavy for too long now. He set the crown on the table and listened to the phone ring.

"Dr. Fowler."

"Hey, Austen. It's Beau. I came by to check on Kylo and he's not doing so great. He's in a lot of pain and running a fever. I made him go to bed, but I don't know."

Austen blew out a breath that brushed the phone. "I worried about this. That was likely a nasty as hell knife. I get the feeling he doesn't rest and let the meds I've given him work without keeping his body stressed. Last night, I left two new bottles of meds for him. Make sure he's been taking those and get some water in him. Give me an hour or so and I'll have a medical team put together for his full-time care. It seems we'll have to make him stay in bed and keep a closer watch. The last thing we need is for sepsis to set in."

Beau nodded along as if Austen could see him. "That sounds good. Send all the bills my way. I'll make sure you're properly compensated."

"It wasn't even a concern. You've always been a good patient."

Beau laughed. One thing he didn't fail at was ensuring people were paid their worth. Austen was damn good at what he did while not seeing a thing. Discreet people were worth their weight in gold. "I'll let the front desk know you're on your way."

"Thanks. I'll get there as soon as I can."

Beau disconnected the call and grabbed the receiver for the security line. They answered on the first ring.

"Security."

"This is floor fifteen." Beau didn't know if that was necessary, but he figured better safe than sorry. "Mr. Jinko is having a health crisis and is expecting a medical team. When they arrive, please send them up."

A pause met his words. "Okay." Another pause. "Please let Kylo know. I hope he gets better soon."

"I will." Beau had no clue who they were, but whatever. Everyone adored Kylo, it seemed. "Thanks for your help." He disconnected the call and picked up the crown. Strangers would be prowling through Kylo's house. He needed to keep it secure. He moved to the safe and easily mimicked Kylo's movements from last night to unlock it. Beau was way more observant than people realized. He locked up the priceless piece and then moved to sit with Kylo. While Beau had no idea why he cared so much, he did. He wouldn't leave Kylo's side. They needed to stick together.

It was too loud for no reason. Shouting pierced his pounding brain. His throat was dry. His eyelids felt heavy. Something pricked his hand.

"Ow." The word was barely a whisper. His voice didn't want to work.

"He doesn't need a goddamn criminal here, endangering his life. You're probably how he ended up this way in the first place. Do you owe someone money? Maybe you did this yourself."

A loud crash had Kylo trying harder to open his eyes. A nurse hovered over him. Another IV hung over his head. "For fuck's sake. What now?" He didn't remember getting stabbed again. No one answered him.

"You've fucked with the wrong one." The screaming seemed to get louder.

Reggie? What the hell? Surely, this was only a nightmare.

An evil-sounding chuckle that sent chills skirting across his skin floated through the air. "The way you flatter yourself. You should go while you can still use both legs. My boys have been bored for a while now. Don't give them a reason to play."

"This is Kylo's home. Only he can put me out."

"Reggie?" Kylo forced the word from his throat, praying no one answered.

His worried face appeared above Kylo, making Kylo's stomach heave. He automatically crossed his arms over his chest, trying to protect his heart. "Why are you here?" Even through a whisper, Kylo heard the fear in his voice. Had he died and gone to hell?

"I saw a medical team headed up, and I followed to check on you. It's a good thing I did. Do you know you have a house full of deadly criminals? Is that how you ended up like this?"

"Oh, God. Please let me wake up."

Reggie grabbed his hand, and everything was suddenly very real. "I've got you."

His heart rate shot through the roof. Machines blared, assaulting his ears. "No!"

Beau appeared like a knight and ripped Reggie away from him. "You're not wanted here. Rico, take care of this. Kylo needs me."

Cursing and arguing continued. All Kylo heard was his blood pulsing in his ears. Suddenly, Beau was there. His face was inches away, and the blaring stopped.

"It's okay. He's gone. Take a breath."

Kylo did as told. He was a good boy. Kylo focused on every detail of Beau to find his way through the panic. "You have beautiful eyes."

A sexy smile met his words. "That's not a compliment I usually get."

The admission had Kylo's head clearing even more. "Why? They're intense but framed by gorgeous lashes. Beautiful."

Beau shook his head. "Do you ever think about yourself?"

Constantly. That was why he was fucking miserable. That was why he hadn't sought help after getting stabbed. Maybe he had just been done, except... this man. There was something about him. Kylo didn't know him and yet he did. He couldn't explain the way he felt when Beau was around. Kylo would swear they had met before and were good friends, but he had never seen the guy before The PlayPen six months ago.

The nurse disappeared. Everything quieted. Beau sat on the edge of the bed and stroked his arms. It felt nice. "Reggie isn't wrong about me. You should throw me out too."

"Mhmm." Kylo closed his eyes and savored the sensation of Beau's hands on his skin. "Well, I have terrible taste, so I think you're good."

A sexy laugh caressed his ears. "I don't know what it is about you. You make me not want to be anywhere else."

The confession made Kylo smile in spite of how bad he felt. "That'll change. Wait until I'm back on my feet. I can be really annoying."

"Maybe that's my kink."

Kylo laughed. He immediately regretted it. He grabbed his stomach. "Ugh. This is not how I pictured seducing you."

Beau's laughter made his dumb words worthwhile. "I'd pay to hear that story, but this is probably not the time. You used all your energy dancing."

He heard the smile in Beau's voice and it was like all was right in the world. The pain didn't matter. His nausea was all but forgotten. It was just them, enjoying each other's company. "So... what's the verdict? Am I dying?"

"Nah. I'd never let that happen. It's just a bad infection and a stubborn patient. You'll be dancing again in no time. For now, rest." He kissed Kylo's cheek.

Kylo grabbed his shirt. Neediness swelled inside him. "Will you hold me, Daddy?"

Beau kissed his cheek again. This time, he lingered. "Let me talk to your medical team and my men. Then I'll hold as you long as you need."

Kylo's fingers relaxed. Beau would be back. Maybe Beau wasn't a good person, like he claimed. Maybe a bad guy was exactly what Kylo needed.

Chapter Four

REGGIE FUCKING FERRIS. BEAU wanted to put his fist through a wall. That was a familiar feeling, but he never expected that guy. Reggie's whole "*he's a criminal*" bit was funny as hell, considering he was a world-renowned piece of shit. Everyone in certain circles knew who the drug dealer to the stars was here. Beau sold guns. Reggie preyed upon people at their weakest. He had called Beau a criminal. Beau couldn't stop laughing about it. Like, what the fuck? Did he think he wasn't?

Kylo padded through the living room to the kitchen. He looked like hell, but also like he had been up and gotten ready for the day. Beau shook his head. His hyper independence exhausted Beau. Beau couldn't even begin to imagine how tired Kylo must be.

"I need to get you a bell or something, so you'll stay in bed and call for help."

Beautiful light blue eyes with dark circles beneath turned his way. "That feels a bit pretentious. I can still walk." He stepped into the kitchen, leaving Beau behind. Then he poked his head back into the living room. "Good morning, by the way."

Beau's cheeks ached, making him realize how big his smile had gotten. He followed Kylo into the kitchen. It was out of his control. Kylo had him on an invisible leash. "You know, I hear hyper independence is a sign of trauma."

Kylo paused in the middle of pouring himself a glass of water. "I read; you know you've finally healed from your trauma when you stop wearing only black." His gaze deliberately dropped to Beau's shirt before meeting his stare again.

Beau couldn't argue. He did always wear black. "Touché."

"Do you want breakfast?"

"I know you're fucking joking." Beau didn't bother to hide his irritation. Kylo was set on killing himself.

Kylo's mouth lifted in one corner. "I planned to order something. You don't want me to cook. I'm a disaster."

"Oh." Beau felt a bit dumb. Kylo had just proven to be so damn difficult. He expected the worst. An idea struck. Kylo had been a lot more open and willing to be cared for while in his playroom. "I noticed a little table and chairs while in your playroom yesterday. Dress however you want and let me order us breakfast. You can just take it easy."

The longing was in his eyes. Kylo wanted what he offered. He twisted his fingers. "You're my guest."

Beau shook his head. "I'm your nurse. Doesn't the nurse usually deliver the food?"

"No. I'm pretty sure the hospital food service people do that."

Beau snorted. "And again, does smart ass-ery win you friends?"

Kylo looked confused for a second. "I'm pretty sure I was just pointing out the obvious. Nurses don't have time for that shit."

Beau took a step forward, invading Kylo's space and backing him against the counter. Kylo never looked away, but his lips parted in surprise. Beau was tired of being disobeyed. "I gave you an order." He touched his lips to Kylo's. Beau planned to brush lips and send Kylo on his way. The neediest shaky breath he had ever heard caressed his ears. He wasn't sure it wasn't his. The next thing he knew, he held Kylo's hair, keeping him in place while he devoured Kylo. He plundered. Beau explored. He kissed Kylo like he was already buried inside him. Desperation poured through him. It had been literally years since he felt genuine passion. Since someone wanted him back. He had to make himself stop. Beau pulled away a hair. "Do as you were told." He swiped another sweet kiss across Kylo's lips.

"Okay, Daddy."

Holy hell. The possessiveness he felt at those whispered words would send Kylo scurrying away if he saw inside Beau's head. "Good boy." He took a step back and pulled out his phone. Beau needed to focus on ordering food. Everything else was unsafe territory. Kylo was in danger. He would see that soon.

Kylo waited patiently in his favorite pink pajamas with the unicorns. He stared at nothing. His mind took turns between going completely blank and seeing an image of a man running around waving a giant red flag. He was in trouble. Kylo recognized all the signs. Yet here he sat, waiting for the trap to snap closed around him. The thing was, unhealthy attention was still attention. As long as it didn't physically hurt, then Kylo would spoon that shit up like a kid in a vat of ice cream. Unless someone had never been loved, they could never understand the lengths a person would go. His lips still tingled from the abuse. God, he wanted to do it again.

"Okay. We have a variety of things." Beau appeared with two bags of food. He sat next to Kylo and went to work, pulling various items out. "We have eggs, sausage, and bacon. There's also fruit and cinnamon rolls."

Kylo's ears perked up at that last one.

Beau obviously didn't miss a thing. He chuckled. "I expect you to eat some real food first."

"I like eggs and fruit too."

"Do you not eat meat?"

"I do, but not anything pork related. It makes me sick. I don't know if it's an actual allergy or anything, but I always pray for death after I eat it."

Beau nodded along, looking like a loving father rather than the man who had wrecked his soul just minutes ago. "Noted." He arranged the food so the eggs were facing Kylo. Beau handed him a fork. "There're all these little packets of seasoning, if you're interested."

Kylo looked through them and added some salt and pepper. He swore he felt Beau's gaze boring into him. A blush creeped up his cheeks. "What?"

"You favor pink. It looks good on you."

Kylo already sat in his secret hideaway wearing pajamas. There was no reason to hold back. "I always preferred girl clothes. My mom, being my mom, let me wear whatever I wanted. She was a firm believer clothes aren't gendered. I imagine she still is, but I'd have to see her to know."

"I hate finding out that *the* Pride Jinko is a shitty mom."

A soft laugh escaped Kylo. "I don't know that she's a shit mom, at least these days anyhow. She's just busy." He heard himself. Despite everything, he loved his mom. He didn't begrudge her any of her fame... except when he did. "And maybe a little self-centered." He flashed Beau a smile. "Maybe I am too, though. I don't know."

"Has she seen how talented you are? You should be on stage."

"I was. Until I wasn't anyhow. I'm sure she knew." Kylo stared at nothing, seeing nothing for a moment, before shaking his head. "It doesn't matter."

"It matters to me. Why aren't you still on stage?"

Gah. His eyes were so gorgeous. He dug too deep. Kylo practically felt Beau burrowing beneath his skin. "I'm too old."

Beau laughed.

Kylo didn't.

Beau's laughter died. "Wait. You're serious."

It hadn't been a question, but Kylo treated it as one. "Very. Ballet is cutthroat. You have to be young, beautiful, and flawless in every way. There's always someone younger and better, waiting to swoop in and push you out. I can't complain, though. Over the years, I've done some of the biggest productions in front of massive crowds. I got to have my Broadway moment. Most people will never say that. Now I just dance for the love of it, in whatever role I want." He motioned toward his crowd of stuffed animals. "With a much smaller audience, of course."

Beau's expression always screamed he saw too much. "I'd love to watch you anytime."

Kylo shoved food in his mouth to hide the hope building inside him. He was more than a little certain he had missed his chance at finding the one. Kylo needed to stop hoping to find his soulmate in every man he met. They had to move on. "Tell me something about you."

Beau chewed and looked thoughtful for a minute. Finally, he shrugged. "You already know I have two sons. Otherwise, there's nothing good about me."

The red flag guy was back. "That's an odd way to state things."

Beau held his stare. "No. It's honesty. You had that crown delivered to me. The only way you pulled that off is if you know who I am. The only good thing I've done in my life is my boys. I don't know if that'll ever change. Maybe I'm every bit as cursed as the crown you gave me."

Kylo's throat swelled. He heard Beau. Despite how things always looked, Kylo wasn't stupid. He just honestly thought he saw something in certain people they didn't see in themselves. Maybe it was real or maybe he only saw what he wanted to see. Either way, he couldn't leave Beau to suffer, and he was. Kylo saw it every time he looked at Beau. It was like looking in a mirror.

Like any wild animal, he had to lure Beau in a little at a time. He acted unbothered by the speech and continued eating. "The night you saved me, you told me your son owns The PlayPen. All I had to do was Google the owner, and I had a last name. With a name, it was nothing to get an address."

Beau still looked entirely too serious. "So you're telling me you know nothing about me except my name and address?"

Kylo smiled. "I didn't say that. That's just how I found you." He took another bite of eggs. "Once I had a name and an address, a ton of news articles were only a click away. Of course, anyone with half a brain cell knows to take most of that stuff with a grain of salt."

Beau had stopped eating. His full focus was locked on Kylo. "You sound unbothered."

Kylo shrugged.

"Why?"

At Beau's pointed question, Kylo set his fork aside. He suddenly wasn't as hungry any longer. "I used to spend a lot of time with Reggie." Even the name hurt his throat. He couldn't talk about this, but it was stupid to stop there. "He never hid anything from me." And his dumb ass thought that made him special.

"Were you two a couple?"

"No." That was definitely true. Kylo was just an idiot.

"He told me you didn't need a criminal here, endangering your life."

Well, he wasn't wrong. Still... "That's rich."

Beau laughed. It was good to see him smile. "Yeah. That was my thought too." He set his fork aside. "Now, do you want a cinnamon roll or do you want to show me your toys?"

Affection washed over Kylo. He was in so much trouble. "Can I do both?"

Beau's dark gaze moved over his face. He turned serious. "I'm pretty sure I'd let you do anything you wanted."

Yep. He didn't stand a single fucking chance. Needy had always been his middle name. Beau looked like just the man to fill him.

CHAPTER FIVE

BANKS: *YOU GOOD? YOU haven't been to the club in a few days.*

Beau: *Yeah. I'll be by later. Something came up.*

Banks: *All right. Just checking in. See you later.*

After a day of sitting still, quietly showing Beau all his toys, Kylo had looked a hell of a lot better. Beau had felt okay about leaving him alone again. The guilt set in almost immediately. Except Beau wasn't so sure it was guilt he experienced. It felt a hell of a lot like he missed Kylo. He needed space to think.

The PlayPen seemed extra busy. Beau sat with his boys. He wanted to be content with that. As he had told Kylo, they were the only good thing he had ever done. Sometimes, he thought he should be proud of the great men he had created, despite his every fuck-up, and walk away. Maybe that was the best way he could show his love. Plus, The PlayPen was just an uncomfortable place for him, and Beau wasn't uncomfortable anywhere. The world bent to him. Not the other way around. Unfortunately, too many people here had seen him weak. His ex was here with his new husband. His only family sat nearby, enjoying their spouses. Beau had never fit. He was the black sheep of the family he created. For years, he had forced dinners with just the boys at their favorite restaurant for a guys' night... and an excuse to be free from the drama at home. He had demanded they come to the house so they could see Tabitha. Beau had pushed, tugged, pulled, and he was fucking tired. He didn't know how to fix this and sometimes he wondered if he should. Maybe they were better off apart. They would never forgive him for all his sins. In his growing anger and frustration, a thought hit. He had never apologized. There were a lot of things he didn't feel bad about. There were even more things he still didn't think he was in the wrong about. But no matter what the world thought of him, Beau loved his kids.

"I'm sorry."

Boone and Banks both stiffened. Their heads turned away from their husbands to focus on him.

Beau couldn't stop now. "It occurs to me I haven't actually said that to you two. You're my sons. I love you both more than anything and I don't know how—"

"Please don't." Beau's teeth snapped together at Boone's angry-sounding interruption. Banks and Boone looked completely closed to him. Boone didn't stop there. "We're trying with you, Dad, but we are not a family who talks things out. That's not a conversation that'll go well for you, so let's just not."

Beau's jaw popped from holding back his temper. The pair looked ready to throw hands rather than speak. They were right.

He wasn't a good person. Beau was the bad guy in everyone's story. There would be no redemption arch for him. He had brought them into this world, provided for them, giving them damn good lives. Beau had done his job. They didn't need him anymore.

The pair went back to watching their husbands. Beau counted slowly to sixty in his head. He wanted a good minute to pass before he excused himself from their lives. That was the apology they deserved. They didn't want to hear about the nightmare of losing their mom to drugs and alcohol decades before she actually died. They didn't want to know what it was like to watch the love of his life turn into someone else and what it was like to live twenty-four hours a day with a raging addict. His bitterness had driven him down a lot of dark roads. He regretted a few of them, but he would never regret being their father. Even if he was done.

Beau opened his mouth to say a quick goodbye. A movement nearby caught his eye. Kylo stood at the mouth of the entrance, looking unsure. He wore teddy bear pajamas with a hot pink tutu. It took Beau a second to realize he wore a huge grin at just the sight of Kylo. Kylo's gaze landed on him. His expression cleared, as if he spotted exactly what he searched for. Every dark thought disappeared as Kylo headed his way. In fact, everything vanished except the adorable man Beau couldn't see anything else from. He wasn't bad in Kylo's eyes. Beau desperately needed him.

Without a single second of hesitation, Beau scooted back his chair and pulled Kylo into his lap as Kylo reached his side. "Hi, baby."

"Hi, Daddy. I hope it's okay for me to be here." He bit his bottom lip, looking guilty. "I don't want to cut into time with your sons."

He was so goddamn happy to see Kylo. "You're not. I'm glad you're here."

Kylo's light blue gaze stayed locked on him, and Beau couldn't look away. He swore he felt Boone's and Banks' stares, but Kylo held him captive with his pure heart. "I didn't know if you'd be here, but I also hated to show up at your door announced. But then I remembered the free passes this guy gave me and I hoped—" His gaze moved toward the boys. "Oh, hey. Hi." He waved at Banks. "That's who gave me the passes. Well, his husband did."

Banks smiled and dipped his chin. "Hello again."

Beau cleared his throat. He hadn't wanted anyone to know Kylo. Beau could never be ashamed of him. He just didn't want Kylo tainted by his world. It was too late now. "That's my son, Banks. He owns the place." He motioned toward Boone. "My other son, Boone." He stroked Kylo's back. "This is Kylo."

They dipped their chins in greeting.

Kylo being Kylo, he never dimmed. "You both look very much like your dad." His gaze moved back to Beau. "I see why you're so proud. They look every bit as amazing as you described." Beau's throat swelled. A huge realization overwhelmed him. He wanted a relationship with his kids, but they didn't want him. Kylo did, and Beau was stupid for holding himself back. Tabitha was gone. He had lost all the battles with every-one in his life a long time ago. It was okay to look toward the future. Kylo was completely oblivious to Beau's inner battles or his sur-render. "I brought coloring books in case you weren't here." He blushed. "I accidentally left them in the car. It would've been kind of awkward if you hadn't been here. I'm not so sure I really fit in."

Beau brought Kylo's hand to his lips and kissed it. "Me either. Would you like to see my home instead?"

Kylo's smile was everything. "Of course." He slipped from Beau's lap, but Beau didn't release his hand. Without looking back, he headed for the door with Kylo at his side.

"Don't you need to say bye to your boys?"

"We've said our goodbyes." Now it was time to stop forcing them to endure his company. Beau wanted to be where he was wanted for once.

With Beau's assurance his car would be fine in The PlayPen parking garage, Kylo rode with him. He was a little nervous today. It had taken all his courage to seek out Beau. Then Beau's sons had been there. Kylo wasn't so sure that first meeting had gone well. The pair had looked at him, totally horrified. That couldn't be good. Now they were headed through a massive iron gate into what could only be described as a compound, and Kylo felt very small. Guards were posted everywhere. It was uncomfortable. There was no hiding from Beau's wealth and power here, or his crimes.

Kylo couldn't say why he was so unbothered by the danger he was probably in. Likely, it was simply years of friendship with Reggie. Since that had nearly gotten him killed, Kylo should be running for his life right now. But Beau looked at him in a way Reggie never had and Kylo was too fucking intrigued to back down. He had always been dumb like that.

They didn't speak. Beau kept him tucked against his side and kissed his hand several times. Kylo lived inside his own mind, trying to decipher every move Beau made. He felt the way Beau's guards meticulously kept their eyes averted, as if they fought against years of training attempting not to stare. He wondered what it was about the situation that left them fascinated. Kylo tended to overthink, though. Likely, Beau had hundreds of men and women he treated the way he did Kylo. Kylo wasn't special. That much he knew.

After parking in a line of expensive cars, guards poured out. The door opened for them and Beau helped him out. It was sweet.

Kylo felt treasured when he was with Beau. He could easily get addicted. That was his biggest fault, really. He got attached to people who didn't feel the same.

Kylo fought to tear his gaze away from Beau to inspect his surroundings. The house was a bit cold, truthfully. It was filled with priceless antiques and artwork. Beau was so much better than a cold museum of a home. Kylo was no stranger to wealth. Beau was so much more interesting than all that.

"I know it's a lot." Beau laughed and looked his way, catching him staring. His smile slipped away. Heat filled his eyes. "You're not one to care about any of this, I know."

Kylo tried to pretend interest in his surroundings. "If you have something you're especially proud for me to see, let me know. Otherwise, I'm just here to be with you." Kylo wouldn't play games. He had done that in the past and it cost him years of his life, getting therapy. From now on, he vowed to be straightforward and honest about his wants. It saved time for everyone involved.

"What does it say about me that I'm not proud of any of this?"

"I don't know. Maybe that you're human and therefore subject to human flaws."

Beau's dark gaze moved over Kylo's face. They stood in the middle of what Kylo assumed was the living room. It was like they couldn't see anything except each other. "You fascinate the fuck out of me."

Beau's softly spoken confession nearly took out Kylo's knees. "Same."

Beau took a step back and glanced around.

Disappointment flooded Kylo's veins. It seemed games were being played after all. Guards stood everywhere, playing witness to his constant rejection.

Beau took his hand and started walking.

Kylo let him drag him through the house. He was too curious about Beau's sudden burst of energy to pull away. Finally, he dipped inside a darkened room. Beau closed the door behind them and Kylo's back hit the inside of the wood that separated them from the rest of the world. Beau's mouth covered his. The zipper on his pajamas slid down and Beau's hands were inside. Kylo tore at Beau's buttons. Fucking suit. There were so many. He lost his patience and went for the pants instead. A moan vibrated around his tongue as his fingers encircled Beau's erection. His feet left the floor. One second, he was against the door. The next, Kylo was on a bed with Beau on top of him. He kept his weight balanced, taking care not to hurt Kylo's wound, even through his lust. Kylo found that sexy as hell. A man who cared for him was definitely his kink.

Beau sat back on his heels and peeled off his jacket. Then he went to work on the shirt. It was dark as hell and Kylo resented the inability to see anything except the bare minimum. He knew Beau's body would be amazing. Everything about him was. A flutter ran through Kylo. It felt so damn good to be wanted.

"I have a feeling I'm missing one hell of a show."

Beau's weight disappeared, stealing his ability to even see his outline. He listened to him moving around. The sound of a belt hitting a wooden floor made Kylo shiver with anticipation. He didn't need to see. His other senses took over.

A bedside lamp fired to life, casting a soft glow. It was obviously a dimming light set to only give off a nightlight level of illumination. It was enough. Beau was nude and digging through the nightstand. Kylo swallowed a moan. Holy hell. He definitely took care of himself. No doubt he couldn't be soft in his profession, but wow. Kylo wanted to touch him.

Beau's gaze swung his way.

Kylo's mind went blank. He had never seen so much dark hunger and it was focused on him. In his heart, Kylo knew he wouldn't walk away the same after Beau.

A condom and lube landed on the bed. Kylo never looked away from Beau as Beau crawled onto the mattress. Kylo let Beau treat him like a doll, methodically undressing him. His hungry gaze never wavered from Kylo. Kylo's eyes burned from him not wanting to blink. He needed to record this memory in his mind clip by clip for playback. It was the sexiest moment of his life. Kylo wanted to hang on to it.

Beau peeled the pajamas and tutu from Kylo and froze. His gaze lifted to hold Kylo's stare. "Did you anticipate ending up in my bed tonight?"

"No." He knew why he asked, though. Kylo wore lacy underwear. He always did.

"Did you plan to try?"

Kylo never broke eye contact. "No." He needed Beau to accept him exactly as he was.

Beau dragged his fingers down Kylo's erection, covered in lace. His gaze followed the motion.

Kylo fought a loud gasp. It felt so fucking amazing to be touched.

"Everything about you is perfect for me." Beau's dark eyes met his gaze. The light danced on the surface of a stare that looked black in the darkness—the devil's eyes. "I want you to belong to me."

Even in the heat of the moment, it felt like an odd thing to say. It was how Beau stated it—like he wanted to actually own Kylo.

Kylo licked his lips, feeling oddly nervous. An awkward chuckle escaped him. "Was that your way of asking me to be your boyfriend?"

"No." His immediate denial nearly sent Kylo scrambling from the bed. He didn't want to be used anymore. Beau immediately froze him in place. "I'm telling you—if you let me touch you like this—you're mine. No one else will ever see you like this again."

He was a goddamn fool because that didn't scare him at all. "Everything about you is perfect for me too."

For a moment, Beau held his stare. Then his underwear was literally ripped away. The fragile lace easily gave way beneath Beau's tug. A gasp fell from his lips and Beau caught it on his tongue. His kiss turned rough to the point of almost violent. Kylo held on and prayed for more. Beau was harsh, yet somehow gentle. He took what he wanted, but it didn't hurt Kylo. His talented kiss kept Kylo distracted as his skilled fingers found his asshole. Wet digits probed and stretched.

Kylo couldn't take it anymore. He had been neglected and rejected for too long. With a firm push, he had Beau on his back. Beau gasped as Kylo took what he wanted and sat on Beau's dick. He froze and took a moment to adjust to the intrusion. Beau's head lifted. His mouth touched Kylo's neck. That was all the encouragement Kylo needed. He used Beau.

"Damn, baby boy. I'm an old man. You're going to kill me. Fuck. Don't stop."

The deep, guttural way Beau said "fuck" nearly made Kylo blow right then. Kylo owned him at that moment. Maybe Beau was deadly and terrifying, but he belonged to Kylo. Kylo took his pleasure and gave it. He put his whole heart into ensuring Beau couldn't look back on any second of their encounter without getting hard.

His side burned, reminding him of his injury.

As if Beau read his mind, Kylo found himself beneath him. He held Kylo and rocked inside him at the perfect angle to protect his wound while ensuring maximum pleasure. Kylo had known he would be talented. Age almost always brought skill.

"Daddy." Kylo heard the pleading in his voice. He didn't care how desperate he sounded. Beau had him on the edge, and Kylo was ready to tear at his skin. He was on the precipice of crying. That was how badly he wanted to blow.

"Daddy has you." Beau stroked Kylo's cock, sending him flying.

A loud cry tore from Kylo, assaulting his ears. Kylo couldn't stop. His hips lifted, leaning into the powerful orgasm.

"Fuck."

The sexy, deep "fuck" took him all the way out this time. Rhythmic whimpers wouldn't stop leaving his lips.

Beau released a loud moan that almost sent Kylo straight into another orgasm. He was real life porn. Beau was a whole-ass show as he came. Kylo simply held on and watched as Beau went through the stages of coming. His face somehow hardened even more than when he had told Kylo he belonged to him. He made sounds that were straight-up hot. Finally, his muscles relaxed. His expression softened, and he held Kylo's stare as he lowered his head. Kylo's throat swelled as the sweetest kiss he ever experienced swiped his lips. If this wasn't real, Kylo wouldn't make it. He had waited and ached for exactly this for too long. Kylo needed someone to love him. Otherwise, he would wither away.

CHAPTER SIX

BEAU COULDN'T SLEEP IF his life depended on it. The steady sound of Kylo's breathing and his warmth on Beau's chest kept his heart in his throat. He had spent so many years immersed in his anger. Beau had lost this. It was peace, contentment, and a seed of something beautiful. That was all Kylo. His light outshone Beau's darkness.

Kylo shifted in his sleep.

Beau closed his eyes. He didn't want Kylo to stay awake because he was.

Kylo kept moving, sneaking from the bed.

Beau peeked open one eye. Kylo practically danced around in place while hunting for something easy to wear. Finally, he snatched up Beau's dress shirt and slipped it on. Beau's breath caught. He was beautiful. Kylo belonged to him. He eyed the room. Beau smiled. He knew he could tell Kylo where to find the bathroom, but he enjoyed watching him without Kylo knowing. Beau nearly gave himself away when Kylo simply started opening doors. He fought a laugh at the second closet he found and the muted growl Kylo released. His heart stopped when he grabbed the next doorknob.

Kylo pulled open the door and froze. For much longer than necessary, Kylo stood in the open doorway. Several nightlights around the room illuminated its purpose. Kylo stepped inside.

There had never been any avoiding this. Beau slipped from the bed and found a pair of pajama pants and followed. He watched Kylo turn in a circle in the center of Adan's old playroom.

Kylo didn't jump when he spotted Beau. He didn't seem surprised at all, but that was Kylo. Nothing seemed to shock him. "I'm not your first Little."

He turned on the light for Kylo. "No." No matter what, Beau wouldn't lie to Kylo. He wanted a life with him. Lives weren't built on falsehoods.

Kylo sat on the swing of the indoor swing set and focused on Beau. "From what I saw online, your wife hasn't been gone long enough to accumulate this much stuff. It had to have taken years."

"Ten, to be exact." He saw all the questions in Kylo's eyes, and he didn't make him ask.

"Yes, I had a lover living in my wife's home. No, she didn't like it. She refused to give me what I wanted, so I refused to give up Adan."

"What did she refuse to do?"

"Get clean."

A sad smile passed over Kylo's lips. "Been there. The only years my mom actually lived with me were the ones at the height of her addiction. I wouldn't wish that on anyone." He glanced around. "I guess this explains why your sons looked horrified by me. No doubt they hate seeing you with another Little after that."

Beau moved deeper into the room and sat on the small coloring table. He knew the large, round table was sturdy enough to hold him. "They're not horrified by you. They just hate me. I've been working on it, but I think I'm wasting my time. Some things can't be fixed. They blame me for their mom's death."

Kylo nodded and then promptly disagreed. "I don't think it's unfixable. Your boys had to know she was an addict. God knows I knew my mom was one."

"I stole Adan from Boone. Then he tried to kill himself, and that still wasn't enough to make me stop punishing everyone."

Kylo's expression gave nothing away. If he thought—like everyone else—that Beau was a piece of shit, he didn't show it. Beau held his breath, expecting anything. Finally, a bitter-sounding laugh escaped Kylo. He stared at nothing. "I tried my ass off to steal Reggie from my mom."

The confession shocked Beau, but only because he hadn't expected it. He had known there was something between Reggie and Kylo, in spite of Kylo saying they had never been a couple. Beau just hadn't decided what it was. He held his breath, hoping Kylo kept going.

Kylo didn't disappoint him. He set the swing in motion, gently moving as he spoke—like comforting himself. "I was a teenager when Mom found herself getting less and less work because of her habit. So I finally had the mom I always wanted, except it wasn't at all what I wanted. She was angry and awful. All the fucking time because she never slept unless she dropped."

Beau didn't want to hear this part. "You don't have to explain. I've lived it."

Kylo nodded. "It's exhausting. If Reggie hadn't come to live with us, I don't know what would've happened. He got her in hand." Kylo stopped swinging and held Beau's stare. "Back then, I didn't know he was her dealer. But you can't make money from a dead addict or one who can't work because they're too fucked up."

"He was Tabitha's too."

Kylo went back to gently swinging. "I'm un-surprised. He owns the habits of the rich. Of course, all I knew back then was some-one showed me an ounce of attention." Kylo looked away. He visibly swallowed, as if try-ing to get himself under control.

Beau decided to give him a minute by mak-ing him feel better about his life. "I begged Tabitha to go to rehab that day. The day everything started with Adan," he explained. "That wasn't an uncommon occurrence, but that day, I was at my breaking point. She threw things and screamed. Told me she hated me." A sad smile tugged at Beau's lips. "I think I already hated her too. Final-ly, she went completely calm and told me to find someone else. She said I obviously found her repulsive since I kept asking her to change. So go get my dick sucked else-where." A bitter laugh fell from Beau's lips. "I was so goddamn done. When I stormed through the house, on my way to do any-thing that got her out of my sight, I found Boone and Adan fighting every bit as hard. I couldn't take it. The noise. The screaming. I was ready to kill someone to make everyone be quiet and take away the constant anger. So I yelled at Boone to get to work and out of my sight. He stormed out, leaving Adan behind."

Beau snorted. "The funny thing was, Adan already practically lived here, and I bare-ly noticed. But that day, I hated everyone, including him. I told him to get out of my house and he laughed. It wasn't a conde-scending laugh. Just a genuine laugh—like he knew I wasn't serious. He asked if he could stay if he let me spank him since he re-ally didn't have anywhere else to go. I don't know why it struck me as funny. Maybe it was just the way he said it, but I laughed, and it felt so fucking good to feel anything except hurt and rage. I thought about Tabitha, telling me to get someone else to suck my dick, and the next thing I knew, I had Adan on his knees. Then Boone caught us. I had ruined two more lives."

Beau swallowed. He should stop with the confessions, but he couldn't. "It felt good. I'd made people hurt the way I did, and I couldn't stop. My wife was an addict and so was my youngest son. Boone had everything because I gave it to him. I just resented the fuck out of every single person I loved. I felt like I had done everything—like no low was too low as long as they got what they wanted. Yet they all acted like..." Beau shrugged. He didn't think he could go on. There was no part of the story where he came out to be the good guy. It just got worse.

"On my sixteenth birthday, I cornered Reggie, and I ended up on my knees." A bitter smile touched Kylo's lips. "He let me because, of course, he did." Kylo stared at nothing. "Again, any amount of attention and I was hooked. I thought that meant I'd won. That had to mean he wanted me and not my junkie mom. I was so stupid." He met Beau's stare. Another acrid smile twisted his lips. "I definitely made a complete ass of myself every single day, trying to be the one he chose. Looking back, I see all the ways he tried to stay away from me." His expression turned dark in a way Beau hadn't thought possible for Kylo. "That is, until I got my first big part and moved into my own place six months later. Even though I was still underage, Mom was just glad to have me gone. One less person around trying to change her. I didn't really see her anymore, but Reggie..."

Beau felt sick because he saw it all. He knew because he was the bad guy. He knew exactly what Reggie's game had been. It was exactly that: a game. Reggie had been an adult, fucking with a kid's head, making him think he was the aggressor. Then he had lost access to his fun once Kylo left. Still, Beau was slightly confused.

"That was a long time ago. Why is he still coming around?" Kylo was thirty-two. He said they had never been a couple. There was more to this.

Kylo shrugged. "You'd have to ask him. I moved from L.A. to New York and then on to San Francisco. He's been around every corner, stalking me, forcing me to find higher and higher security."

"Stalking you." Fuck. He had to be brutally obsessed with Kylo for it to have lasted this long.

Kylo suddenly stopped swinging. He looked haunted. "I wish it had only been stalking."

Beau came to his feet. He didn't even realize it happened. "What else has it been?"

Kylo focused on him. He looked like the child no one protected. "He's hired people to attack me, hoping to scare me into running to him. The week before we met at The PlayPen, I was held hostage for three days until he came to my rescue." Kylo used air quotes on the word "rescue." They were unnecessary. Reggie obviously didn't care if Kylo saw his ploys for what they were. Kylo took a shaky breath. "I think he paid that guy to stab me." Kylo stood. "Where's the bathroom?"

Beau held his hand out for Kylo. The moment he held some part of him, his feet unglued from the floor. "This way." He led Kylo to the opposite side of his bedroom. After opening the door and turning on the light, he stepped aside, leaving Kylo to his privacy. Except, once the door closed, he couldn't move away. No one had watched over Kylo. No one had protected him. Beau had never protected anyone. In fact, he was the monster. But Kylo needed him in a way no one ever had, and Beau planned to deliver. He was a little terrified of himself at that moment. An image of Reggie's expression as he had stood over Kylo's bed floated through Beau's mind. Kylo was right. Reggie had done that, and Beau didn't know what horrible thing he was about to do about it, but he knew it would be irreparable.

After splashing water on his face, Kylo stared at himself in the mirror. He wasn't a kid anymore. None of that shit mattered. He closed his eyes. The memory of Beau's lips on his skin washed away the darkness. The honesty. Goddamn. Beau hadn't held back or tried to lie about a single thing. He had flayed himself in two and let Kylo stamp through the remnants. That was the single most touching thing anyone ever did for him. Kylo didn't have to guess around Beau. All he had to do was ask, and Beau ripped out his heart for Kylo. He wanted to hold him.

Kylo turned off the light and opened the door to find Beau waiting. Even with his eyes still adjusting to the change in lighting, he knew Beau was in a dark place. He didn't have to study his expression. Beau swept him off his feet.

"Bedtime. Do you need a story?"

God. He could love this man. "No. I think I've had my fill of stories tonight. I think I just need to be cuddled."

"You got it." He crawled onto the bed and tucked Kylo beneath the covers before slipping beneath them too. Beau towed Kylo into his arms and held on.

Kylo closed his eyes and savored the sensation of being held. His eyes burned. His heart couldn't get enough.

Beau kissed his forehead. "I hate to ask you to rip your heart out any more tonight, but did Reggie give you that crown?"

Sadness threatened to sink him again. "No. My mom gave it to me for my eighteenth birthday. It wasn't a coincidence that it had been made for a son a king couldn't love. I'm a son a queen can't love, and she wanted me to know it. But hey, it's worth millions, right?"

"What made you wear it the night we met?"

"I've worn it every birthday since. It's my yearly reminder not to bother."

Warm lips touched his forehead again. This time, they didn't move away, even when Beau responded. "At least I got you a gift." Kylo appreciated Beau not adding those roses and teddy bear hadn't been meant for him.

An unexpected chuckle burst from Kylo. He fucking adored this man. Still, he had to stand his ground. He wouldn't lose himself again. "I don't want the brightly colored prison you built for Adan."

"I'll have someone clear out the playroom tomorrow."

"If you think you'll be touching anyone other than me, plan to lose your hands."

He felt Beau smile against his skin. "You don't have anything to worry about. I'm crazy. Not stupid."

Kylo's cheeks ached. Beau kept him smiling. "I'm crazy too. Fair warning."

"Good. I can give you a gun and you can be my Clyde or whatever."

"Wouldn't that make you Bonnie?"

Beau laughed. It was a soft and sexy sound. "I don't know. I'm ridiculous when I'm tired."

Kylo snuggled in even closer and kissed Beau's neck. "Go to sleep, gorgeous. I'll keep you safe without a gun. My hands are deadly."

He felt Beau shake with silent laughter and—somehow—Kylo's smile got bigger. Maybe they were two fucked-up peas in a pod, but they had each other. That was enough for Kylo.

CHAPTER SEVEN

THE HARD WAY KYLO slept told Beau exactly how much Kylo still needed to heal. He left the bed, showered, and dressed. Beau sent someone to get flowers for Kylo for when he woke up. He arranged them next to the bed and had Pierre on standby to feed Kylo when he finally dragged himself downstairs. Kylo slept through it all without budging.

Henry appeared at his side as Beau reached the bottom of the stairs. He knew Beau. They made a good team. "SUV?"

"Yes. We're picking up a few people?"

"Ah. The Yukon."

Beau chuckled. Yeah. Henry knew him. The Yukon could hold up to nine people. He definitely needed that today. While Henry headed for the garage, Beau found Mickey.

Mickey's green eyes swung Beau's way at his approach. "What's up, boss?"

"Kylo is still sleeping. When he wakes up, don't let him leave. Tell him Pierre will be sad if he doesn't eat the special meal he's cooked for him. Say whatever it takes to get him to stay. He's not safe outside this house." He hesitated. Beau didn't usually explain himself, but he was trying to be a new person. "Reggie hired that guy to stab him. I don't want Kylo out of our sight until this is fixed."

Mickey looked thunderous. "Don't worry. I got this while you take care of that guy.

Fucking Reggie," Mickey muttered under his breath, making Beau smile.

He felt like he was on the right track. Beau motioned for Rico to come with him. They piled into the SUV and headed for The PlayPen. Beau had already checked with his connection. His sons were there. Fewer trips were best, and this wasn't the type of thing he could discuss anywhere but the safety of Banks' club. Still, his impatience made the ride feel like it took forever. He nearly growled in relief when Henry dropped him at the door. Rico watched his back as they headed inside. He must have looked exactly how he felt because Boone and Banks went on alert the moment they spotted him.

He didn't waste time. "Leave Shane to watch your boys. I need you to come with me." They stood without question and moved to let their husbands know. Adan's husband sat at the table, looking bored and ignoring Beau. Beau felt nothing for Adan or him, except a fondness for the friendship they gave his sons. "You want in on this too?"

Axton's eerie light gaze focused on him. He looked like the killer he was. "Where you headed?"

"To kill a pedophile."

Axton stood. "Let me tell Adan to stay close to Shane until I get back."

Beau dipped his chin. Something stirred in his chest. He had fucked up more in his life than most people did in ten lifetimes, and still these men didn't hesitate to back him. It was more loyalty than he deserved, but he hoped to earn it someday. But today, Beau needed to be the bastard who took the west coast weapons trade by force. Beau was a lot of things, and his moral compass was practically zero, but he was no groomer. He wouldn't allow one to live who had harmed one of his. An evil smile tugged at his lips. Just ask Adan's uncle. Oops. Not possible without a seance.

In under ten minutes, he had his boys loaded into the SUV. They rode in silence for much longer than he could stand. He needed to warn them about what they were headed into.

"You should know. I'm going after Reggie."

No one seemed surprised to hear he was a child groomer.

Boone nodded. "Good."

Beau fought a smile. They might have their issues, but they always had each other's backs. It was more than most could say.

Kylo took himself on a tour of the house while he waited for Beau's return. Mickey hadn't mentioned where Beau had gone and his cageyness on the matter said Kylo was probably better off not knowing. With a general idea, thanks to Pierre, of what areas of the house to avoid, he wandered aimlessly. He left the employees' quarters alone. There were so many rooms. A majority were obviously unused. It didn't take him long to get bored and move back to the kitchen, seeking company.

Mickey smiled at his appearance. "You want some coffee?"

Kylo sat at the table with him. "No, thank you. Another cup and I'll be bouncing off the walls."

"That's okay. No one will judge."

He had nice green eyes. They had laugh lines around them. That said a lot about how happy of a person he was. "How long have you worked for Beau?"

Mickey looked thoughtful, as if adding years in his head. "About twenty years, I guess."

That answer took Kylo by surprise. "What? Did you start working here at ten?"

Mickey laughed, nearly spewing coffee since Kylo caught him mid drink. "Seventeen."

Kylo hated that he was being so nosey, but he didn't stop. "You don't look thirty-seven, but seventeen? That's awful young to become someone's bodyguard."

"I didn't start as that." He chuckled and shook his head, as if recalling something funny. "Beau saved me from the streets. He likes to pretend he kidnapped and enlisted a possible witness to one of his crimes, but you have to let someone like Beau keep their hardened reputation."

"Kidnapped? This sounds like a story I need to hear."

Mickey shrugged. "It's not that exciting. I was just one of the many homeless teens who ended up here. In my case, I was in an alley, tagging a building." Mickey laughed again, as if he couldn't believe he had once been a dumb teen, doing dumb teen stuff. "There was a black SUV parked nearby. I kept glancing its way, because it was definitely out of place for the rough neighborhood. Suddenly, these guys in suits poured out, and I was kindly asked to get in the car, except it clearly wasn't a request, you know? I had no idea what would happen, but I was pretty sure I was dead if I got in that SUV. Unfortunately, there were way more of them than me and they had guns, so I got in the vehicle. Apparently, Beau was there to do business, and I was in the wrong place at the right time. Since it was very possible I had seen stuff I shouldn't have, my choices were join up or die." Mickey stared at nothing for a second before continuing. "The funny thing is, I've thought about that day more times than I can count. I don't think any deal went down. I think Beau just saved me."

Kylo's chest warmed. Beau was such an enigma. He was happy they met. Kylo opened his mouth to dig for more, and the door flew open. A blood-covered Banks rushed inside, looking wild-eyed.

Mickey was on his feet in an instant. "Where?"

"In the SUV."

Mickey was racing through the house before the words died on Banks' lips. Kylo was right behind him with his heart in throat and a chant running through his mind. Please don't let it be Beau. It was Beau. He froze in his tracks as Boone and Henry carried Beau inside. Blood was everywhere. He couldn't get a good look at Beau with him surrounded by people. A guy with long, platinum hair held pressure on a wound. He was pale and obviously in shock.

The guy's gaze landed on Mickey as Mickey danced around, obviously looking for a way to help. "He took a bullet for me. Why would he do that?"

Kylo took a breath. Beau needed him. "Get him upstairs. Mickey, go get Austen. Break every speed limit."

Mickey nodded and was out the door.

"Someone needs to get Jupiter. I can't—" Boone was obviously on the edge of hyperventilating.

"Who is Jupiter?"

Boone focused on him. He looked like Kylo's question gave him a much needed grounding point. "My husband. He's at The PlayPen with Kyson and Adan."

Kylo nearly flinched at hearing Adan's name. Now wasn't the time to question if it was Beau's Adan. It didn't matter. Kylo focused on another guard he didn't know. "Go to The PlayPen and pick up the Littles. Take them to Adan's playroom when you get back. They don't need to see this." With orders in place, Kylo followed everyone upstairs to the same bed where Beau had made love to him. That was where Kylo got his first good look at Beau. He was awake but visibly gritting his teeth. Kylo didn't hesitate to climb on the bed and sit by his head so he could run his fingers through his hair.

"Hey, baby." Beau sounded totally calm for someone who likely had next to no blood left... if all this was his.

"Did you have a busy day?"

Beau tried to laugh and ended up wincing.

Kylo shushed him. "Don't listen to me. You know I get weirder when I'm stressed."

"I love that about you."

"Dr. Fowler is on his way. You didn't have to try to outdo me."

Beau wore a huge smile despite his circumstances. "I have to show you what's it like to deal with a terrible patient who won't relax. It's only fair."

Kylo glanced up for a second, hoping to see the doctor rush through the door. Everyone stared at them—like they couldn't believe their eyes. Kylo dismissed them and went back to focusing on Beau. He kissed his forehead. His lips lingered. Kylo couldn't pull away. He was so fucking scared. They had just found each other.

"Don't be scared. I'll never leave you."

Kylo swallowed past the lump in his throat at Beau's promise. Beau needed him to be strong. "I know, because I'd dig you up and kick your ass."

He heard Beau's weak chuckle.

"Mickey, Henry, and Rico. You three can stay." Kylo's head shot up at the barked order. Austen was there. He looked ready to go to battle. "Boone and Banks, get cleaned up. I might need you too. This might take a while, and I need people who are rested. Kylo, there's a room full of Littles next door. They're scared and confused. You're the steadiest person I know. They need you."

Kylo wanted to argue that Beau needed him more, but he knew Austen tried to protect him from reality. Beau was in bad shape. Still, he didn't budge. If Beau didn't make it, Kylo would be at his side until the end.

"Please, baby. My sons-in-law aren't as brave as you are. I'll feel better knowing you're with them."

He was torn. Kylo didn't give a shit about these people he didn't know. Beau mattered to him.

"Please." Beau held his stare.

Kylo knew this was a man who didn't use that word often. He nodded. "Okay, Daddy." He pressed a kiss to Beau's lips and forced himself from the bed. His legs didn't want to hold him on his walk to the playroom, but he knew he had to be brave. It was what Beau wanted.

CHAPTER EIGHT

A LOUD SILENCE WAITED for Kylo inside the playroom. At his first look at the three men dressed in pajamas, Kylo knew Beau was right. Two of them looked terrified. The third comforted the blood-soaked platinum-blond from earlier.

Kylo closed the door, hiding the carnage from view. He slowly moved to the coloring table where everyone sat and claimed a chair. Kylo took a breath. He focused on the blond. "Tell me what happened."

"Who are you?" The pretty brunette dressed as a cat didn't sound as catty as his outfit. He merely sounded upset and confused.

"My name is Kylo. Beau and I..." He trailed off because he didn't know what to call them. They had established they were exclusive, but he didn't have a title for them.

"He's your daddy."

At the brunette's claim, Kylo nodded. "What's your name?"

"I'm Adan." Of course he was. He was fucking flawless. Kylo had never felt more lacking in his life. Adan stroked the blond's hair—who was still obviously in shock. "This is my husband, Axton."

"I'm Jupiter. Boone's husband," Jupiter said, pulling Kylo's gaze his way.

Kylo dipped his chin and focused on the last Little, the only one he recognized. "Kyson, right? Banks' husband? You gave me a few guest passes to The PlayPen a while back when we met at a library story hour."

Kyson nodded. "It's good to see you."

Kylo forced a smile to his lips. "You too." He looked around. "It's really nice to meet all of you. I hate that it's under these circumstances." Kylo focused on Axton. "Earlier, you said he took a bullet for you. Will you please tell me what happened?"

Axton swallowed. His eerie light eyes looked more confused than anything. Of course, he also looked hardened by life, so Kylo didn't have a good read on him. "Beau came by The PlayPen this morning and asked if we wanted to join him to hunt down a pedophile."

Kylo's heart sank. He had a bad feeling he knew where this was headed.

Axton kept going. "Beau and I don't get alo ng... for obvious reasons," he said, motioning Adan's way and looking uncomfortable for the first time.

Kylo stiffened his backbone. "I know the story. It's fine." He wasn't sure he actually knew anything, but he needed Axton to keep going, and he didn't currently give a shit about their story.

Axton nodded. "Anyhow, as soon as I heard where he was headed, our past didn't matter. I'm always down to do some ratchet shit for the right reasons." A small smile appeared on Adan's lips and Kylo swore he felt the love between them. He felt oddly close to Adan in that moment—like they were somehow connected by their ability to see past a hard man's faults.

Axton shook his head. "I don't really know what happened. It's like they knew we were coming. The second we rolled from the vehicle, bullets were flying. One second, I was halfway out of the SUV, and the next, Beau shoved me to the ground." Axton shallowed. "He took a shot that should've killed me. Why would he do that?"

Kylo knew in his heart he would regret asking, but he had to know. "Who was Beau after?"

"Reggie Ferris. He's a big-time drug dealer in this area. Beau said he had let the guy live too long, but now he knew Reggie had groomed a child and he couldn't let that stand."

Kyson snorted. "That's rich."

Kylo's gaze shot toward Kyson. "How so?" Even though he thought he might be sick, knowing Beau had gotten shot going after Reggie because of him, he didn't like Kyson's insinuation.

Kyson motioned silently toward Adan.

Kylo's gaze shot Adan's way.

Adan took an audibly tired-sounding breath. "Okay, guys. We have to talk about this. More than anything, I want to be friends and leave my past in the past. But that'll never truly happen until we speak candidly about my and Beau's relationship. Maybe you don't see it, but I feel like this is constantly hanging over my head and in the back of everyone's mind. Now isn't the time, but this is something that needs to be said for my peace." He took another deep breath. This one sounded like it hurt. "I was never a child."

Kylo's heart dropped at the statement because he knew what that meant. He had been that kid.

Adan kept going with a strength Kylo didn't possess. "Not for a day, as far back as I can remember, was I ever a child."

Kylo's eyes fell closed. He had at least been much older than that. There were so many child molesters in the world, ripping away the years of innocence everyone deserved.

After clearing his throat, Adan pressed on. "When I met Boone, I was fucked up. It probably doesn't matter to anyone else, especially Boone, and I know it excuses nothing I've done, but I was fucked up." Adan said the words with his whole chest—like he couldn't stress enough how bad his mental health had been. He kept going, proving how strong he was now. "Maybe I had finally made it to adulthood, but my soul didn't. I don't think I truly loved anyone, especially myself. All my buttons were set to self-destruct, and I didn't care who I took with me. Whatever it took to not feel anything, that's what I did." His eyes suddenly filled with tears, and he visibly swallowed. "That's not Beau's fault. In fact, I think he was in the same boat for different reasons, and it was so much easier to be fucked up with someone who couldn't judge me. Boone had always only known love. He didn't and couldn't understand what it looked like inside my head. It still kills me, knowing how much pain I caused, and I can never fix it. All I can do is be better. But please stop hating Beau on my behalf, because it only makes me feel twice as guilty. If you can't let go of anything else he's done, there's nothing I can do about that, but his relationship with me was on both of us. I'll never feel like we're truly friends until you see me for who I really am. I was a victim, but I wasn't Beau's victim. If anything, this gilded cage..." He motioned around the room. "It was my moment to breathe and heal from things no child should ever endure. Without those years, I could've never found the real love I have now."

Kylo didn't care they were sitting in the play-room built for this man who Beau once ob-viously cared about, maybe even loved. He couldn't watch anyone hurt the way he saw Adan hurting. Kylo stood and hugged Adan. He half expected to get shoved away. To his surprise, Adan hugged him back—like he truly needed Kylo's embrace.

Adan touched his lips to Kylo's ear and whis-pered, keeping his words private. "I can see you really love him. You have no idea how badly he needs that. Thank you. For his sons' sake, thank you."

Kylo's eyes burned with unshed tears. He pulled away and swiped at them on the sly. Kylo moved away from the family while they continued their candid discussion that had obviously been needed for a long time. He hoped they would continue to heal, and one day Beau had his kids back because of this open conversation. Right now, all he could think about was Beau and whatever was happening on the other side of the playroom door. He had never felt more alone, and that was saying a lot. All these people, they had someone. Past issues or not, they were sticking together. As always, Kylo just had himself.

Adan was the first one to wrap his arms around him. Then Jupiter and Kyson joined in. Kylo couldn't say what happened. He simply fell apart. Kylo ugly cried and he couldn't stop. His entire life, Kylo had faced everything alone. Beau had given him someone to lean on for the first time and he might lose him as quickly as he found him. The worst part was knowing it was his fault. He had gone after Reggie for him. Once again, Reggie had taken from him. It couldn't stand. Reggie had better be dead. If not, he would be. Kylo would make sure of it.

Austen was exhausted in ways they hadn't invented words for yet. Back-to-back emergencies kept hitting him. He never dreamed it would be so hard to keep the rich alive, but goddamn. They were always up to some shit, from drug overdoses to getting shot. He was one man doing the work of twenty. Austen just wanted a nap. Unfortunately, it wouldn't happen anytime soon.

He found Kylo sitting alone in the kitchen and staring at nothing. Kylo jumped slightly when Austen set his hand on his shoulder. Pretty blue eyes focused on him. Another one who got away because Austen worked too much and couldn't pursue him the way he wanted.

"He's sleeping, but I feel certain he'll pull through."

Kylo's shoulders sagged. "Thank you. You're a miracle worker."

A sad smile pulled at Austen's lips. He wished that wasn't all he was. It got old existing for no other reason. "You should probably rest."

Kylo nodded. "I know, but I was just waiting to hear how Beau is doing before I take care of something."

Austen grabbed a chair and sat. He didn't like the dark look in Kylo's eyes. "I just stitched you back together. Whatever you're thinking, please let it go. This has to stop somewhere."

A wry smile passed over Kylo's lips. "Why does everyone think I'm weak?"

Austen snorted. "No one who saw you after getting attacked could possibly think that. Beau will need you here when he wakes up and he'll kill me if he finds out I knew you planned to do something stupid, and I did nothing to stop it."

"Then come with me."

The instant horror couldn't be hidden.

Kylo laughed at his expression. "How long will it be before Beau wakes up?"

"Likely hours."

"Good." Kylo stood. "You can come with me, or I can go alone. It makes no difference to me."

"This is dumb, Kylo. Reggie already almost killed Beau. You know he'll be on high alert, watching for someone to come after him in retribution. Let this go for the night."

"I'm not going to see Reggie. I have a different errand to run."

Relief washed over Austen. As long as they weren't going after Reggie, he could spare a little time for Kylo. "Oh. Okay. Sure, I guess. I don't think you should go anywhere alone right now."

With a nod, Kylo took Austen's hand and pulled him to his feet. He grabbed a gun and a set of car keys from the kitchen island. "Let's find out what these go to."

Austen groaned. Kylo would definitely get him killed, especially if this trip was anywhere other than to get ice cream. He doubted as much since Kylo worked to hide the gun, which he definitely shouldn't need, inside his teddy bear pajamas. Still, he got in a car with the guy and put on his seatbelt like a goddamn idiot.

They didn't speak on the drive. The radio stayed silent. Despite his dread, Austen dozed. The exhaustion beat him. Finally, Kylo stopped in front of an unmarked building.

"Stay behind me." Kylo climbed from the car before Austen could argue.

"For fuck's sake." Austen followed. He couldn't believe he was doing this. Even though he didn't exactly know what Kylo planned, there was an odd feeling in his gut. It wasn't precisely dread. He couldn't explain it.

Upbeat music poured from the building when Kylo pulled open the door. The place was too well lit inside to be a nightclub. Plus, it looked totally dead. They rounded the corner and Austen found himself staring at a dance studio. It was obviously private. There were no signs marking the building.

"Knock. Knock."

Austen thought Kylo's greeting went unheard until the lone man inside danced their way. He couldn't look away. Austen had never seen a man so delicate and beautiful. His every move was flawless and light—like he floated through the air. His bright green eyes held an innocence that made Austen feel like he should straighten his clothes and make sure his hair didn't stand on end.

The man's gaze locked on Austen, holding him captivated, but he headed for Kylo. "My butterfly." He had an accent Austen couldn't place, but it weakened Austen's knees.

Kylo got pulled into the man's dance. Together, they made the most gorgeous couple he had ever seen. Austen couldn't even blink. He had never been so mesmerized. Their dance slowed and Kylo spoke close to the other man's ear. Then Austen watched the guy kiss Kylo and say something that stayed between them. For a moment, they stared at each other so lovingly, it swelled Austen's throat. Then Kylo's dance ended at Austen's side. Before Austen saw it coming, he spun across the floor in the arms of his mystery man. For a moment, he simply allowed himself to be swept around the room before coming to his senses.

Finally, he managed to make his mouth work. "I'm Austen."

"Rain."

"Beautiful." Even Austen didn't know if he meant the name or the man. It didn't matter. It was both.

Rain's mouth lifted in one corner. He left Austen at Kylo's side. They held each other's gaze. Austen couldn't breathe. He didn't know what happened to his brain, but it was fuzzy. There was also something going on with his breathing.

"You'll see me again." With that promise from Rain hanging between them, he turned away, leaving Austen floored.

Somehow, Austen found himself buckled in the car and halfway to Beau's place. He finally managed to unglue his tongue from the roof of his mouth. "Who was that?"

The silence that followed his question had Austen giving up on learning the answer. Then Kylo shattered his world. "That was the deadliest assassin in the western world and he's about to kill Reggie for me."

Well, fuck. Austen was more aroused than he had ever been in his life.

CHAPTER NINE

As MUCH AS BEAU would have loved to teach Kylo a lesson about dealing with bad patients, Kylo never allowed it. Allow might be a strong term. It was more like Kylo made Beau want to do everything Kylo asked. He had no desire to leave the bed until Kylo lured him into slow walks to get back his strength. Then they would be right back to bed. Kylo stayed with him. They watched movies, which Beau hadn't really done in years. Kylo showed him funny videos on his phone. He set up bedside visits with Beau's sons. One day, Beau even got to enjoy a fashion show after Beau ordered a ton of pretty things for Kylo. He wanted Kylo to have all the lace. Unfortunately, it got a little harder every day not to make love to his angel. Still, he loved falling asleep every night with Kylo in his arms. Love was becoming a familiar theme in his thoughts. He always thought he wouldn't feel that evil emotion again. It didn't seem love cared what he thought.

In a short, pink lace robe and sheer lace underwear, Kylo sat on Beau's thighs and checked his bandages.

On his back, Beau watched, hard as a rock and dying inside. He ran his hands up Kylo's thighs. A sweet smile touched Kylo's lips, but his gaze never wavered from its task. Beau snagged the satin belt on the robe and tugged, untying the piece. The two halves fell apart, giving Beau a better view of the body he adored.

"It's a little scary how easily you control me. A sexy outfit and the right seat and I'm yours to do with as you like."

Kylo's smile grew. "Why scary?" His gaze finally met Beau's. "I'd never use my powers for evil."

Beau hauled Kylo higher so he could feel how badly Beau wanted him. "I'd argue you already are. I'm dying to be inside you."

Kylo leaned forward and braced his palms on either side of Beau's head. The lace of his robe tickled Beau's skin, adding to the torture. "If I thought for a second you'd let me have complete control, so you're not straining in any way, I'd give you whatever you wanted."

Beau's fingertips slipped beneath Kylo's thong, skimming his crack. "I can be very good when properly motivated."

A heavy knock sounded, making Beau growl. Kylo dropped his forehead onto Beau's shoulder for a second before rolling from the bed. Beau wadded up the comforter and pulled it higher to hide his erection. He didn't allow anyone entry until he fully enjoyed the show of Kylo heading inside the bathroom. Damn. Beau didn't want to be good.

"Come in."

Henry strolled in all smiles. "Hey, boss. You're looking better. Kylo is doing a great job of getting you back up and on your feet."

He was up all right. "He's the perfect nurse. What's up?"

"I just wanted to give a bit of a report, which is none whatsoever really. There's still no sign of Reggie. It's like the bastard disappeared from the planet."

Beau blew out a tired breath. "Okay. I won't feel safe letting Kylo out of my sight again until I know he's dead. It's looking less and less likely he plans to resurface."

Henry nodded. "He has to know he's dead if he ever shows his face again, and not in a quick and easy way."

Beau's gaze slid toward the bathroom. If he could get Henry out of here, he could go on the hunt.

Henry must have taken the hint. He cleared his throat. "Well, I'll let you get back to resting." He was out of the room strangely fast.

Kylo poked his head out the door. "Is he gone?"

"Yeah. He practically ran for it. I think he sensed he was interrupting."

Kylo stepped from the bathroom and locked the bedroom door.

Beau's hopes rose, especially since Kylo's underwear was missing. Only the robe remained. Beau tossed the covers aside, letting Kylo see he was still hard.

Kylo stood over him and tapped his chin. "Those pajama pants look uncomfortable. Maybe I should strip you."

"Agreed." There was no missing the hunger in Beau's voice.

A naughty look flashed his way as Kylo stole Beau's clothes. "I may or may not have slipped in a lube bead while I hid."

"Good boy."

Kylo straddled his thighs again.

Beau tried tugging the satin belt loose again.

Kylo stopped him by holding tightly to the belt. "Not so fast. Your word."

Beau played dumb. "What do you mean?"

"No moving. I have total control."

There was nothing Beau wouldn't promise to get to enjoy Kylo. "I'm yours to do with as you please."

With a nod of satisfaction, Kylo reached past him to the nightstand. Beau grabbed his arm, stopping him. "What if we skip that?" Beau desperately wanted to feel the effects of that bead without anything in between, but he also needed to know this was it for them. They were forever.

Kylo's gaze moved over Beau's face. "What are you really asking for here?"

He should have known Kylo would never be anything but straightforward. "I'm saying this is it for us. Forever."

Kylo's expression was hot as hell. The lust was in his eyes and riding on his cheeks. His fingers lightly caressed Beau's erection. He shifted positions. Kylo held his stare. "Do you want to fill me with cum, Daddy?"

He was going to die. Kylo would kill him. There was no way he could stay still through this, but he would damn well try. "Good boys drip for their daddies."

Kylo's tight heat engulfed him. Beau almost broke his word immediately. His body wanted to jackknife from the bed. The gunshot wound that cost him his spleen screamed for him to stay still.

He tugged the satin belt, exposing the body he craved all hours of the day. "Damn. Daddy's pretty little boy looks like he needs someone to touch him between the legs."

Kylo tilted his chin up and sucked air when Beau stroked his cock while he bounced on Beau's dick.

"That's it, pretty princess. Nobody else makes Daddy feel like you do. You're perfect."

Kylo whimpered, and Beau fought the urge to throw him down and fuck him hard. He could turn that small whimper into a scream.

"Goddamn. That tight little asshole is Daddy's favorite game to play. Show me how it flutters when I pet you here." He squeezed Kylo's erection.

"Daddy. I need…" His whimpers turned desperate.

"I'm so fucking in love with you."

Kylo blew as Beau made the confession, but his entire body froze. He held Beau's stare, looking shocked into silence. Beau was a bit surprised too. He hadn't meant to say that, but he wouldn't take it back. They had taken turns pulling each other from the edge of death. This was real. They had seen each other's worst, and it was the best thing that had ever happened to Beau.

Despite all that, at the moment, all Beau knew was the way Kylo's body milked him. His brain glitched and his muscles tried to snap as he fought not to move while ecstasy rocked him. He couldn't stop gasping for air. He wasn't sure he wasn't on the edge of a stroke. Beau didn't think it could get better or his orgasm harder. Then Kylo proved him wrong.

"I love you, Daddy."

"Fuck." The deep guttural curse came from his soul as he pumped Kylo full of cum. In a flash of clarity—like his life flashing before his eyes—Beau saw the future. They would always have each other's backs. This was the relationship he had suffered to get to. Kylo was the one. Beau never wanted to look away again.

Kylo's insides shook. Sometimes being with Beau could be so fucking intense. It wasn't about the sex, even though that was pretty damn soul-rocking. It was just Beau. He was larger than life. Beau had something that couldn't be defined. Being in his presence was extreme. It was like being inches from a tiger... except that tiger loved him. He was loved. It was paralyzing. Love always left him.

"Talk to me."

Kylo stroked Beau's stomach while he listened to Beau's heartbeat. "I'm just being weird."

Beau rolled.

A growl burst from Kylo. "What are you doing? You'll hurt yourself."

"Hush."

Kylo huffed at the admonishment but did as told.

Beau stroked his face and ran his fingers through Kylo's hair. "You're worthy of love."

Tears immediately filled Kylo's eyes. He had to look away from the sexy dark stare that saw too much. For once, Beau's intensity was too overwhelming. The eyes that saw into people's soul saw too deeply today. "So my therapist says."

Beau kissed the corner of his mouth. "Stop that. Unless you want to call me a liar."

Kylo's gaze snapped back to hold Beau's stare. "I wouldn't do that. You're the most wonderful and honest person I've ever met. In fact, that's what I fell for about you. No matter what, you tell me the truth. That's such a rarity."

"Then listen to me." He swiped another sweet kiss across Kylo's lips. "You're—" Beau stopped suddenly and turned inward. A small smile played on his lips before he seemed to come back to himself. "You're like that first breath after thinking you'd drown. That's where I was before you danced into my life. There was no air. Then you literally swept in and brought sound and color back to my life. You make me want to just stop and sit with you. For the rest of my life, I just want to hold you and beg you to see how much I fucking need you."

Tears freely streamed from Kylo's eyes and slid back into his hair. The lump in his throat felt like it choked the life from him. "I'm scared as hell of losing the version of you I'm holding right now. I don't think I can stand to have another person give me a crown."

He hoped Beau understood what he meant. Kylo didn't know how else to explain the terror of having love replaced by things. He needed this to be real, normal, and healthy.

Kylo felt Beau's body melt. It was like something relaxed inside him that even he hadn't known he held rigid. A small smile touched his lips and disappeared as quickly. "I never wanted to say this, especially in a moment like this, but yeah. That terrifies me too. There was a time when I had a wife and kids. A normal life with Christmas mornings and love. I watched it slip away and found out the hard way it had never been real. After the addiction really sank in, and I found myself on my knees begging for her to get help, Tabitha admitted she had never loved me. She married me because her parents forced her, and then she had stayed for the money."

Kylo's heart broke for Beau. "That was probably the drugs talking."

Beau shook his head. "It wasn't. She loved our kids and the life we built, but I wasn't someone she could love. Even before I built this empire, I was the person who could be this man. The things I'm willing to do to not go back to my childhood, to not have my kids ever know starvation, those weren't traits she could love." A soft chuckle fell from Beau's lips. It sent chills skirting down Kylo's spine. "That's rich, since she stayed married for money. I never could figure out how she thought she was better. But the sad part was, I still loved her. My side was real. So I couldn't let go. I just knew if I could get her clean, then I could make her love me. Just like I had built this empire brick by brick, I could bend her feelings to my will. I guess, every time it didn't happen, it was my pride that couldn't take it. I didn't want the world to know she had made a fool out of me. So I made a fool out of her instead."

Kylo knew all the way to his soul he was the only person to ever know the real reason for Adan. Maybe Beau had hoped for a second the move would break Tabitha's addiction. That her not wanting to look like an idiot would outweigh the hold drugs had on her. But that hope had turned to bitterness, and Kylo got it. Deep down, he knew that was the real reason he had been so susceptible to Reggie. It was spite. He had wanted his mom to look like a fool. Kylo wanted her to hurt the way she hurt him.

"We are so ridiculously alike. I've never been this close to fate. It's looks damn beautiful from here."

"Yeah. It does." Beau's gaze moved over Kylo's face. When he spoke again, his voice came out in a broken whisper. "Hi. I've been waiting a really long time for you."

The tears immediately returned. Kylo nodded. "Same."

Beau kissed him. He lingered on Kylo's lips. Their feet played and time passed around them. Beau was still in bed, healing, so Kylo could live with this pastime. He supposed Beau had been ready to leave the bed for a few days now. It was Kylo's fear that kept him there. Beau had let him keep him down so he could feel secure about Beau's health. Damn. He was wonderful. Kylo wasn't dumb. He knew this was a version of Beau no one else saw and likely didn't even believe existed. That was what made them even more special to Kylo. Not only did someone finally love him, Kylo knew no one could take it from him. Beau was too strong of a person, and he had chosen Kylo. Miracles never ceased.

CHAPTER TEN

THE MONTHS KYLO LIVED with Beau were the best of his life. There were also always people around. He was never fully alone. For some people, that might have driven them crazy. Kylo adored knowing there was always a beautiful soul around the corner. Then there was Beau. There were no words. He was loved and accepted. It was beautiful. Kylo had slowly let the past slip away. He sold his penthouse and quit calling his mom. Kylo gave up hoping she would love him. She had actually called him a couple of times, which shocked him, but progress, he supposed.

"You have great cheekbones. An artist's dream."

Mickey laughed. "Maybe don't say that. You'll get me killed."

Kylo chuckled as he moved closer to the canvas, trying to get Mickey's eyes perfect. "Beau knows I'd never do a single thing to hurt him and that I love all art forms. He would never want me to stop seeing the beauty in the world."

"Good. That's definitely a trait needed in this house. Everyone loves how you're slowly turning every shared space into a home again. Tabitha intentionally made the place colder, trying to spend as much money as possible to drain Beau while making him feel like this wasn't a place he could relax." Mickey paused. "I shouldn't have said that.

You don't want to hear about any of that, and Beau would not love me saying anything."

Kylo stopped painting to focus on Mickey. "It's okay. I don't want anyone to feel like they have to watch their every word. This is your home. It wouldn't be fair of me at all to act like Beau didn't exist before he met me. So don't watch your words."

Mickey's mouth lifted in one corner. He shook his head. "I don't think he did exist before you. Not really."

Kylo's throat swelled. These guys always left him touched by their kindness. They didn't know what they did for him. His life had been so quiet and empty. Now it was full of light and smiles.

Kylo patted Mickey's arm. "Thank you for being you." He went back to painting. Beau had asked him to stay downstairs while he had workers clearing out Adan's old playroom. Kylo felt a little bad now for asking for that. Beau had waited so long to have it done, Kylo thought he had forgotten, and Kylo had let it go. Since meeting Adan, he didn't feel the same. But all those toys should go to Adan. They were his. Then again, Adan might not want any of his past mucking up his future. Kylo never knew if he made any right decisions, but he tried. There was a point in his life he couldn't say that. Beau made him better in a hundred ways. They made each other better. That was real love. He was so goddamn grateful for it. Kylo would never take this new family for granted.

With his shoulder leaned against the door-frame, Beau watched Kylo paint. A tiny smile kept playing on Beau's lips. He tried wiping it away, but it was Kylo. His uniqueness was irresistible. Dressed in a schoolgirl outfit with purple bows in his hair, he was flawless. Kylo was born to be exactly as he was. Beau couldn't love him more. He straightened.

"Can I steal you, baby?"

Mickey immediately stood. "Sorry, boss."

Beau fought a laugh. He knew that was bullshit. "Why? You're doing exactly what I pay you to do."

Mickey hid a smile when Kylo wasn't looking.

Kylo looked up from his painting. "Hey, Daddy. Sure." He set his paintbrush aside and focused on Mickey. "Thank you for humoring me."

"Of course. It's been fun."

Beau's affection grew for Mickey a little more every day. He was the perfect guard for Kylo. Henry had been right to suggest him for the position. Kylo didn't even realize he was being protected. He did a wonderful job of keeping Kylo entertained and oblivious, to Beau's surprise.

Beau held his hand out as Kylo crossed the room. "I have something to show you."

Kylo linked fingers with him. His smile never dimmed. "Really? What?"

Beau clucked his tongue. "Nope. You have to wait and see."

"A surprise?"

"Yep."

Kylo skipped a little. "Yay."

While Beau led Kylo to the bedroom, he kept sneaking glances Kylo's way. He was all smiles—like pure sunshine. Beau had never breathed so freely.

When he stopped Kylo outside the door separating their bedroom from the old play-room, Kylo protested. "You don't have to prove to me it's empty. I should've never asked you to do that. I could've just com-bined my toys with what was already there and let it go. It was a ridiculous request."

Beau waited until Kylo got that out of his system before speaking his piece. "Yes, I did have to do it, because I need the space for this." He opened the door, revealing the transformed room.

The dance floor gleamed, and mirrors cov-ered the walls. Kylo's stuffed animal audience waited for his next performance with a few new stuffie additions. A music system gave Kylo access to any song he could want. Kylo stood frozen with his hand over his mouth.

"Oh my god." The muffled words came from behind his hand. His eyes were full of tears when they swung Beau's way. "I can't believe you did this."

With a smirk, Beau strolled into the room and moved to the sound system. He started the song he had already chosen before going downstairs. He picked up Kylo's ballet shoes and held them out. "Would you dance for Daddy?"

Kylo didn't hesitate. With a tiny squeak, he ran Beau's way and snatched the slippers. He plopped down on the floor and put them on. In no time, he spun around the room. His skirt flew upward, spinning with him and showing off his pretty pink underwear. Beau sat and enjoyed the show. He had never felt peace before Kylo. Not really. He had spent every minute of his life scraping for more and more power and money. Those things had been the only real company he had. But Kylo was his peace. He completed Beau.

Kylo did a final leap, pulling off the move flawlessly. He stood in the middle of the dance floor, looking happy, and like Beau's everything. Beau had waited for this moment for what felt like his entire life.

He came to his feet and crossed the room.

Kylo watched him with his heart in his eyes.

The next song flowed from the speakers. A love song.

Kylo reached for him. "Dance with me, Daddy."

For a moment, he simply held Kylo without moving before he answered. "In a moment, baby. First, I need to ask you something." Beau dropped to one knee and held out the ring he had been carrying around. He had known he would know the perfect moment when he saw it. This was it. "Will you marry me?"

Kylo blinked a few times. "Holy crap. If I were you, I'd be terrified of marriage."

A bark of laughter burst from Beau.

Kylo snatched the ring from the box. "Lucky you, I'm not you." Kylo couldn't do anything normal. He put the ring on and urged Beau to his feet. "I can't believe you want to marry me. Every time I think you can't do anything more to floor me, here you are, and you're wearing a pink shirt today."

"It's salmon." Beau had no idea what that had to do with anything, but he didn't imagine he would ever figure out how Kylo's brain worked.

"Either way, it's not black. That means you're healing."

Beau could not stop smiling. "How could I not? I have you."

Kylo's expression turned serious again. "You're the best gift I've ever gotten. Thank you."

"Don't thank me. Just let me keep you."

Kylo shuffled close and tucked himself against Beau. Beau held him and their feet automatically moved with the slow music. With Kylo's head tucked beneath his chin, Beau fought the emotions overwhelming him. The backs of his eyes burned with un-shed tears. He held the most precious thing he had ever possessed. Beau made a silent vow to be the best man Kylo could possibly ask for... in the ways he knew how. Beau fully intended to keep Kylo in this lifestyle he deserved. No matter what he had to do.

Beau kissed Kylo's head. "I love you. I love you so fucking much."

Kylo held him tighter. "I love you too. You'll be the happiest husband ever. I promise."

"I know, baby." He already was the happiest man alive. They couldn't fail.

Chapter Eleven

Lake Tahoe looked amazing this time of year. It made for a beautiful backdrop for the archway where Beau stood. His gaze moved over his guards. They were posted in all the obvious places, dressed to the nines. Beau was grateful for them. Even though Kylo and he had decided to marry in private, Beau appreciated someone being there—employees or not. In the eight months since he had gotten shot, Beau had seen his sons more, but he didn't think they would ever be a normal family. Beau definitely didn't think they would come to this wedding. While they seemed to like Kylo, any time he left them alone, and then returned, the room would be dead silent. There was no missing the way they carefully avoided speaking or even looking at each other. He hated that, but Kylo made him happier than he had known he could be. Beau wouldn't lose this while his boys lived their own happy lives. They were grown. It was his time.

The music began, and Beau turned. A huge tent had been erected to keep Kylo out of sight until the right time. Beau held his breath. His heart rate kicked up a notch. A tiny part of him still feared this wasn't real. The tent flaps opened and his attorney, Jarek, stepped out with his husband Luca on his arm. Jarek wore a knowing smile as he moved to stand off to the side, exactly like he intended to stay for the ceremony.

"What—"

The flaps moved again before Beau could finish his question. Adan and Axton stepped out, confusing Beau even more. This felt like an intervention, and he was not in the mood for anyone to ruin his wedding. Again, before he could say a word, Shane and Soren appeared with Boone and Jupiter close on their heels. Banks and Kyson filed out behind them. Everyone wore matching shit-eating grins. It hit him. They were there for the wedding. Before he decided how to respond, Kylo stepped out. Beau forgot to breathe. He couldn't see anyone or anything except the wildly dressed man heading his way. He wore pajamas that looked like a tuxedo, along with a tutu that was black-and-white striped. Kylo was the most beautiful sight Beau had ever seen. His face hurt from smiling. He felt lighter than ever before. Then Kylo stood at his side. They faced each other. Their gazes never wavered. "You did this."

A sweet smile touched Kylo's lips. "I know you were afraid they wouldn't come if we invited them. That's a blow you couldn't handle. But I knew they would be here for you. So I decided it would be a cute surprise for you."

His heart climbed into his throat. "Thank you for this. You have the most gorgeous heart I've ever seen. I couldn't love you more."

Kylo looked proud of pulling off his surprise. Thankfully, Beau had something up his sleeve too. Hopefully, he wouldn't be the only one of them moved today.

"Shall we begin?"

They gave each other a sharp nod and faced the officiant at the question. Beau hung on every word. He wanted to remember every oath and vow. For once in his life, no one would break the relationship he held above all others. They both spoke clearly as they repeated every word they were asked to repeat. The ring on his ring finger felt familiar, yet lighter than the last one he had worn. It felt real—like it meant something this time.

"I understand you had a special request for this part of the ceremony."

Kylo looked confused at the officiator's statement. "What did you do?"

Beau smirked. "You're not the only person who can plot." Beau motioned for Henry. "I want this marriage to be a true fresh start for us. No ugly pasts or curses."

Two identical crowns appeared.

Kylo's eyes widened. He looked between them. "Is this—"

"One of them is." Beau's smile grew. "Neither of us will ever know which one is the original." He took one from Henry and placed it on Kylo's head. "No one is more loved than you, baby boy. You'll always be my king and my heart. My husband and family. Best friend. Forever."

While wearing a huge grin, Kylo accepted the second crown from Henry. Henry smiled like he was the one getting married as Kylo placed the crown on Beau's head. "King Daddy. I've never regretted putting this crown on your head that first time. Now I can't wait to pull it out once a year and eat cake while wearing our matching crowns until the day we die. Then I swear I'll find you in the next life and the next. You won't ever hurt again."

"I now pronounce you husbands. You may kiss."

Beau's throat was too swollen to speak, but the rest of him still worked. He had Kylo towed against him in an instant. Their lips met. The kiss quickly turned heated—like no one watched them. Beau heard the clapping and congratulations. He didn't see anyone except Kylo. He never thought this would be his life. Sometimes he would still get scared it wasn't. He half expected it to fall apart, but Kylo never so much as sipped wine. Beau knew Kylo wouldn't let him down and become the person Tabitha had become. Some fears simply lived too deep to ever completely disappear. The happiness in his soul went even deeper than the terror. He knew this was the love he had waited his entire life to find. It was too beautiful to be anything else.

Kylo absolutely adored that he had gotten the drop on Beau by arranging for his family and friends to be there. Beau cared more about others than he wanted them to know, and Kylo knew it killed him not to have his sons around. Kylo got it. Being hard kept Beau alive. He had Kylo now to watch his back. Beau could let his guard down a little.

While sitting in Beau's lap, they took turns feeding each other cake. Lively conversation went on around them. The boys playfully argued over something neither wanted to take the blame for as teens. Some sort of destruction of property. Kylo barely listened. His entire focus was on Beau's touch.

"I still can't believe you did this."

Kylo shrugged. "When you said you wanted it to be just us, I saw your expression. You didn't want that. I couldn't let you settle. But wow, did you make it difficult. I barely got a second alone with anyone to plan. Every time we got into the details, you'd pop right back into the room. Then you didn't want to have the tent, and I thought I would lose my mind."

"The tent is a security issue. I only have so many guards I trust to cover such a large area. Reggie might've dropped off the map, but I know he's biding his time. Our wedding is exactly the type of thing he'd want to destroy."

Kylo bit his lip. A hint of guilt over holding his tongue wormed its way through him.

"What?" Beau leaned back and eyed him. "I know that guilty look. What did you do?"

Kylo winced. "I might've had a friend of mine make him disappear."

Beau blinked. "What?"

The shock written in Beau's every line might have been funny any other time. Kylo flashed a guilty smile.

"Please excuse us." Beau stood and carried Kylo from the reception area they had rented. He checked room after room until he found what looked like an unused dressing room for events. Beau set him on a bench built into the wall in front of a mirror. "Spill."

He looked so stern. Kylo twisted his fingers, panicking a bit. They had just married. He couldn't lose him already. "When I was part of a big production in L.A., my co-lead was a guy named Rain Agafonov."

Beau's eyebrows rose.

Kylo wasn't surprised Beau had heard of him. "By your reaction, I assume you know his other career."

"Uh, yeah. I thought the guy was a ghost no one knew how to find. Most people don't just visit an assassin."

Kylo shrugged. "He's my friend. Anyhow, Reggie kept showing up at every performance and it always upset me. Rain kind of joked that he would make Reggie disappear if I wanted. At the time, I laughed it off. But then, after a show one night, we were headed home. Rain and I always parked next to each other and walked each other to the car at night. Anyhow, we were headed to the parking lot and these three huge guys came from nowhere. I just sort of stood there frozen while all three men seemed to drop dead around me, and Rain wasn't even out of breath afterward. I hugged him so hard, still thinking he somehow just reacted out of fight or flight. He kind of just rubbed my back and told me not to worry about a thing. Rain told me to go home and wait for him. He'd be there soon, and we'd talk, but for me not to talk to anyone else before he got there. I did, and he showed up a few hours later. We talked until the sun came up. It was a very eye-opening discussion. I finally realized he had been serious about Reggie because I never heard a thing about those men again. We stayed friends even after the production ended. Over the years, we've been in other shows together. Strangely, I forgot all about that night until you were shot. I didn't know if you'd live, and I was out of my head." Kylo shrugged. "I just kind of got in the car and drove to his place. We spoke, and I told him I was ready to take him up on his offer." Kylo's hands rose and fell. "Just as he promised, Reggie vanished."

He didn't like Beau's expression. Kylo couldn't read him. Panic rose in his chest. Every second he got closer and closer to hyperventilating. Before he could stop it, a tear escaped him.

"Please don't be mad at me, Daddy. I just couldn't deal with Reggie anymore. He tried to take you from me. I couldn't let him."

Beau swiped away the tear that rolled down Kylo's cheek. "I'm not angry, baby. You just caught me off guard. You should've told me sooner, so I didn't waste my men's time." He looked thoughtful for a moment. "And Rain Agafonov is a hell of a wildcard for my back pocket."

"No." Kylo didn't mean to sound so hard, but this was a firm line for him. "Rain is off limits. He's my friend. Nobody will be using him. He's been used enough in his life. He deserves peace. I wouldn't have gone to him if I hadn't been desperate." Even Kylo heard how distressed he sounded. He couldn't stop it. He loved Beau, but he couldn't let Beau try to use Rain for his own gain.

"Okay. It's okay. Just take a breath." Beau went down on his haunches, getting on Kylo's level, trying to calm him. The move made Kylo realize exactly how upset he had gotten. "I'm sorry. If you say no, I'll always listen. Okay?"

Kylo nodded. "Okay." He took a breath. "Thank you. Rain means a lot to me. I don't want to ruin our friendship."

Unexpectedly, Beau shook his head and laughed. "Rain Agafonov. Reggie Ferris. No fucking wonder you didn't even flinch when you learned who I am. God, you're the bravest and strongest person I know. I love you so much."

Everything inside Kylo warmed. "I love you too. Being your husband is the best thing that's ever happened to me."

Beau shifted to his knees and inched closer. His hands ran up Kylo's thighs. "What will your mom say when she finds out you got married and didn't tell her until afterward?"

Kylo shrugged. "I don't know. Our gift from her will be nice, though, I'm sure."

Beau shook his head again. His expression changed, turning heated. His fingers walked their way to the zipper of Kylo's pajamas. Kylo's cock stirred as he slowly slid it down. His mouth went dry. Beau was incredibly sexual. He might have been the older one, but he kept Kylo fed and exhausted.

"We have guests."

Beau smirked. "I guess you'd better come quickly, then." He hauled Kylo closer. He had Kylo's dick out and in his mouth in seconds. Kylo gripped the edge of the bench and sucked in a ragged breath as his erection hit the back of Beau's throat. The sight of his sexy silver fox bobbing on his cock had Kylo racing toward the edge. Dark eyes that saw all the way to his soul focused on Kylo. A stuttered breath burst from him. Lust and love filled him to the point of painful. He bit back a cry as he blew on Beau's tongue so fast it was almost embarrassing. Even just over a year ago, Kylo couldn't picture a life like this. That suffocating loneliness that he lived with every day felt like a million years ago. He knew that was Beau's doing. Each and every day, Beau woke up and worked for them. He drowned Kylo in attention and love. Kylo was determined he would always do the same for his king. Maybe that crown wasn't cursed after all. It had brought them together in a way nothing else could. He might owe his mom a phone call after all. Fate had shown up and out for them. Kylo would never stop being grateful. He had found heaven.

Austen's book is the first book in a new series, Killers Inc. It's called *Dancer*. Even though he's been in a few of my books, you don't have to read any of them to enjoy the new series. Mickey and Henry will also be in the new series.

About the Author

CHARITY PARKERSON IS AN award-winning and multi-published author with several companies. Born with no filter from her brain to her mouth, she decided to take this odd quirk and insert it in her characters. One of her greatest loves is writing morally gray characters. You'll find them scattered throughout her hundreds of titles.

*Nine-time Readers' Favorite Award Winner

*2015 Passionate Plume Award Finalist

*2013 Reviewers' Choice Award Winner

*2012 ARRA Finalist for Favorite Paranormal Romance

*Five-time winner of The Mistress of the Darkpath

Connect with her online:

*Sign up for her newsletter: https://bit.ly/charityparkersonnewsletter

*Join her readers' group on Facebook: http://bit.ly/CharitysTribe

*Website: https://www.charityparkerson.com

*A list of her social media accounts and giveaways all in one place: http://hy.page/charityparkerson